Outbid by the Boss

Outbid by the Boss

STEPHANIE BROWNING

Copyright and Publishing Information

Outbid by the Boss
ISBN eBook: 978-0-9938299-0-1
ISBN Print edition: 978-1-950402-04-5
Copyright © 2014 by Anne Stephenson and Susan Brown
Publication Date: July 15, 2014

Undone by the Star
ISBN eBook: 978-0-9938299-3-2
ISBN Print edition: 978-1-950402-05-2
Copyright © 2016 by Anne Stephenson and Susan Brown
Publication Date: April 5, 2016

Making Up is Hard to Do
ISBN eBook: 978-0-9938299-8-7
ISBN Print edition: 978-0-9938299-9-4
Copyright © 2018 by Anne Stephenson and Susan Brown
Publication Date: March 28, 2018

All rights reserved. Except for use in any review, the reproduction or utilization of this work in whole or in part in any form by any electronic, mechanical or other means, now known or hereafter invented, including xerography, photocopying and recording, or in any information storage or retrieval system is forbidden without the written permission of the author.

This is a work of fiction. Names, characters, places and incidents are either the product of the author's imagination or are used fictitiously, and any resemblance to actual persons, living or dead, business establishments, events or locales is entirely coincidental.

Cover and Interior Design: Heather McIntyre
Cover&Layout, www.coverandlayout.com
Cover Photography: @nd3000

Outbid by the Boss

Books by Anne Stephenson and Susan Brown

Writing as Stephanie Browning

Outbid by the Boss
Undone by the Star
Making Up is Hard to Do

The Amber and Elliot Mysteries

The Mad Hacker
Something's Fishy at Ash Lake

www.susanbrownwrites.com
www.annestephensonwriter.com

Contents

Chapter One
Chapter Two
Chapter Three
Chapter Four
Chapter Five
Chapter Six
Chapter Seven
Chapter Eight
Chapter Nine
Chapter Ten

A Sneak Peek at:
UNDONE BY THE STAR
MAKING UP IS HARD TO DO

About the Author

One

Two thousand pounds!

A trickle of cold sweat worked its way down Samantha Redfern's ribcage and lodged itself in the waistband of her well-worn jeans. Two minutes ago, she'd been the only one bidding on a rare, 18th-century candlestick and now some yahoo she couldn't even see at the back of the auction hall had managed to double the stakes in less than half the time.

No matter. Tucking a stubborn strand of auburn hair behind her ear, Sam scanned the other bidders. Antique silver was her area of expertise. It had won her a coveted position with Burton-Porter & Sons, and now here she was, moments away from owning a piece of the past. Her past. And nothing, not even an amateur collector with more money than brains, was going to stop her now. All she had to do was stay calm.

"I have two thousand pounds…" called the auctioneer. His practised gaze rested on Sam for the briefest of seconds before moving on in search of wealthier prey "…do I hear two thousand, one hundred…"

What was she waiting for? She'd been searching for a candlestick exactly like this since she'd first arrived in England and this one had it all…London hallmarks, date marked 1749, manufactured by a well-known silversmith, and rumoured to be part of a larger collection once belonging to the king himself.

It was a wonder half of London hadn't shown up to bid on it. She'd known about the candlestick since she was a child growing up in Toronto. A family secret, her grandmother had told her. Sam frowned. Maybe not so secret after all…

"….going once….going twice…"

"Come on, lovey!" The middle-aged woman in the seat beside Sam gave her a jab and up shot Sam's hand, startling both her and the auctioneer.

"I have two-thousand, one hundred pounds!" he crowed. "Do I hear two-thousand, two?"

The auctioneer, Sam thought, was having way too much fun.

While she decidedly was not.

A flood of guilt washed over her. She should so not be here. She should be in New York City. Attending an important sale on behalf of her London employer. Not perched on the edge of a folding wooden chair in a cramped auction hall in a teeny, tiny village in the West Midlands that, while very picturesque, belonged on top of a biscuit tin. Her colleagues at Burton-Porter wouldn't believe it. They saw her as the consummate professional. Cool as a cucumber, that's me, thought Sam, as she wiped her damp palms along her thighs.

An excited buzz rippled through the room. The phantom bidder had just upped the ante by another hundred pounds. Sam twisted in her seat, trying to catch a glimpse of her competitor, but there were too many bodies in the way.

She swung back to find everyone watching her, waiting to see what she would do. "I have two thousand, two hundred pounds," the auctioneer repeated. "Do I hear three….?" he asked looking directly at Sam.

This was absolutely crazy. Her budget was stretched to the max. She was living in a central London flat so small, she could barely bend over the sink to brush her teeth without butting up against the shower door. And the bidding had already soared past her credit limit.

Maybe if she sat on her hands…

"Going once…."

"….going twice…."

It was no good, thought Sam raising her hand one more time.

She just had to have it.

The auctioneer acknowledged her bid with a twitch of his moustache. "I have two thousand, three hundred pounds. Do I hear four?" he peered down the length of the room.

Sam held her breath.

Please, please, please, don't bid.

He didn't, and the next thing she heard was the smack of the auctioneer's gavel. "Sold to the young lady in the second row for two thousand, three hundred pounds."

Sam leapt to her feet, green eyes sparkling in triumph. She tossed her bag over her shoulder, gave her neighbour a hug and set off, hurriedly picking her way through the tangle of legs and carry-alls to the end of the row.

With her long hair caught up in a clip and her favourite blazer topping jeans and boots, Sam strode towards the rear of the building to pay her bill and pick up her prize. It was the happiest she'd felt since wrangling her way to England.

If everything went according to plan, she would have just enough time to swing by the flat with the candlestick. Her suitcases were in the car, she'd downloaded her boarding pass that morning, all she had to do was drop off the rental and catch the shuttle to the airport.

It was going to be tight, but totally worth the risk.

The candlestick was hers!

From where he stood, leaning against an immense mahogany armoire, thirty-six-year-old Chas Porter had a clear view of Samantha Redfern as she bounded down the length of the hall.

What was she doing here?

And why would she be bidding against him?

Unless... Chas shook his head. No, that was crazy. She couldn't possibly have known his interest in the candlestick. Or that the auction house had tipped him off before the sale.

At first, he hadn't even recognized the young woman bidding against him. He'd arrived late and been unable to get a seat, but his commanding height had ensured his bid was noticed. And allowed him to see his opponent.

In the office, Miss Redfern's hair was always neatly pulled back. Not threatening to spring from its pins into a shoulder-length wave of shining auburn. In London, her clothes were boringly routine, charcoal grey and conservative, if he remembered correctly, which suited her position as a buyer for one of the country's most exclusive dealers, but did little to enhance her physical appeal. Soft voice, an unexpected uptilt of her chin when a valuation she had made was questioned – he had barely noticed her.

Until now.

Chas pulled out his mobile. If she'd wanted his attention, attending an out-of-the-way sale when she should be in New York, was a sure-fire way to get it. Sending a quick text to his office confirmed it. Samantha Redfern had been booked to fly out last night, but had rescheduled.

Simmering with rage, Chas sliced his way through the thick crowd, nodding to a few familiar faces and avoiding those who knew him well. That his employee was at a country auction bidding on his candlestick when she should be on the other side of the Atlantic preparing for one of the season's most important sales was beyond belief.

He could hear the auctioneer in the background clamouring for the crowd's attention – a Royal Crown Derby tea set was on offer, but Chas' focus was all on the Sam. In the time she'd been with Burton-Porter, he'd found her totally professional and decidedly aloof. Which was more than okay with him.

Never ever dip your pen in company ink, his grandmother had drummed into his teenaged ears.

As the great-great grandson of the firm's founder, she scolded, having heard he was chatting up a female employee in the accounting department, he should know better than to play off his connections. Young, romantic, and hot-headed, Chas had ignored his grandmother's advice, until the day he heard the young woman bragging to her co-workers. It was his wealth and position they saw, his grandmother told him sharply, not the man he was. From that day on, Chas had guarded himself against all but the most casual relationships, ruthlessly channelling his excess passion into his work. Over the years, he had been able to rebuild what his father and grandfather had squandered.

His eyes narrowed. And no one, not even a trusted employee like Samantha Redfern, was going to jeopardize that success.

The spring in her step was unmistakable as she wove her way towards the cash. What was it about this particular candlestick, Chas wondered, and this particular employee?

Despite her knowledge of antique silver, it would be impossible for Samantha Redfern to make the connection to his family. Or would it? She was smart, she was ambitious and, Chas scowled, for all he knew, quite prepared to exploit any advantage that might come her way.

Barrelling through a knot of onlookers, Chas came to a halt. She had reached the cash desk. He was a few feet behind her now, but instead of seething with fury, he found himself admiring the view.

The fitted jacket and tight jeans she wore revealed the lush curves that had remained hidden at the office. His usual taste ran to the elegant, slim, society women who understood how to play the game, not to employees who promised a cosy armful. Irritated by his own thoughts, Chas shook off this sudden flash of warmth and refocused his attention on why she was here and, for that matter, why he had let her outbid him!

She stood with her back to him, wallet open, tapping the wooden floor with the toe of her high-heeled boot until the auctioneer's assistant set her prize on the battered oak table.

The candlestick was in superb condition.

Just under nine inches in height with a circular base, swirling shell motifs rising up its stem and a petal-shaped lip surrounding the socket. In a London sale, he would expect it to sell for another five hundred pounds. At least. A pair wouldn't just double the price, it would triple it.

His gaze slid back to Sam.

He should be pleased that he'd hired one of the best eyes in the business, but knowing she wasn't there on behalf of the firm any more than he was, rather tarnished his high opinion. But why would she risk her position with Burton-Porter on this particular candlestick?

Chas felt a slow smile tug at the corners of his mouth. This scene unfolding in front of him was about to get interesting.

Not knowing the sale's payment policy, Samantha Redfern was waving a credit card about. The equivalent of a red flag as far as country auctioneers were concerned.

The auctioneer's wife took one look at Sam's credit card and said, "Cash or cheque."

"I'm sorry?" said Sam.

The woman jabbed her pen backwards to where a dog-eared sign hung limply on the back wall. "Cash or cheque," she repeated.

"Debit," countered Sam. She selected a bank card from her wallet and held it up for inspection. "As good as cash…"

The pen pumped the air one more time. "Read the sign."

"But this is an auction," Sam stammered. "I go to them all the time…"

"Look," the woman said quietly, "there are half-a-dozen people behind you waiting to pay. Either you come up with the cash or the item will be offered to the next bidder." Her grey eyes slid over Sam's shoulder and landed on Chas, flickered in recognition and then moved on when Chas shook his head.

He could almost hear Sam's heart beat faster. In the salerooms, her only giveaway when she was tense or dealing with him, was a gentle pulse near the soft skin of her left temple.

Maybe it was time to tap her on the shoulder and identify himself as the other bidder. The candlestick would be his. As it should have been in the first place. Although she was pushing her luck on the New York trip, she was one of the best silver appraisers he'd ever hired. Maybe he'd overlook this one.

At least, he might have, had Samantha Redfern not pulled a white envelope embossed with the Burton-Porter logo from the depths of her shoulder bag.

"Do you take American?" Sam asked.

"No."

It was all Chas could do not to reach out and grab his errant employee by the scruff of her slender neck. Instead he found himself sidetracked by the silky curls that had escaped her hair clip.

"Please…I have more than enough cash and…" Sam rifled through her wallet. "…I can do at least a third of it in pounds." She had dumped her entire bag onto the table and was pawing through its contents as if her life depended on it. "I'll pay the bank premium."

Dark brows furrowed, Chas watched her toss aside a pair of designer sunglasses, her mobile, a half-eaten chocolate bar, a neon-pink cosmetic bag and what looked to be a balled up pair of black tights. He saw no sign of a cheque book, but he did see a set of car keys with a familiar tag.

When Sam finally found what she'd been hunting for, a small change purse with an even smaller cache of banknotes, everything else went back in her bag. Everything except the envelope with the American cash.

"All right then..." the auctioneer's wife was muttering as she made her calculations. Sam glanced at the total, removed a wad of hundred-dollar bills, and handed it over.

The deal was done.

"Thank you, thank you, *thank you*," Chas heard Sam say as she lovingly scooped up the candlestick. "You have no idea how much this means to me."

"It's not me you should be thanking," drawled the woman. Her eyes slid past Sam's.

But Chas Porter was already beating a retreat through the crowded hall – this was not the place to confront Miss Redfern no matter how much she deserved it.

Clutching the candlestick to her chest, Sam

hurried for the exit. She had a plane to catch. And now, she realized with a frisson of panic, she not only had to nip back to her flat, she also had to stop at the bank. It would take all her savings and half her rent money to replace the firm's cash, but her purchase was worth every penny.

As she dashed through the open doorway, Sam remembered thinking how nice it was that the morning rain had given way to a sun-filled afternoon and then…

Woof!

She ran smack into a wall of solid masculinity, gasping as the base of the candlestick dug into her ribcage.

She staggered backwards. A pair of strong hands grabbed her upper arms to steady her, holding her fast as she regained her balance.

And then he spoke.

The "thank-you" Sam was about to utter caught in her throat.

"In a hurry, are we?" The voice was well-bred, well-schooled and awfully familiar.

She squeezed her eyes shut.

And began to mentally chant.

Please, please, please…anybody but Chas bloody Porter. Please, please, please…

"Anytime…" the voice said, rudely interrupting her pleas to the goddess of single women caught in compromising positions.

Stupid woman must be on a lunch break, thought Sam.

Her lids fluttered open and she followed the buttons of the beautifully-stitched, pale-blue oxford-cloth shirt he wore beneath his soft leather jacket to the button at the base of his neck. It was open. Revealing enough of the man to make one feel that every inch of him would be just as enticing as the dark stubble on his chin, the slightly battered but still patrician nose and…the steel-blue eyes washing over her like an icy Arctic wind.

"Miss Redfern, isn't it?" Chas Porter said, his voice dripping with sarcasm. "I could have sworn you were representing us in New York this week. You do remember the two-day sale at Sotheby's? Previews in….what?" He removed his left hand and checked his watch. "Twenty-four hours?"

"Which, allowing for the time change," replied Sam, choking back an urge to flee, "gives me twenty-nine hours…

"Now, if you don't mind…" She pointedly eyed the hand grasping her left bicep, an amazing feat given the fact that her knees had turned to water and her brain was sending high-pitched alarm signals to every nerve in her body.

Chas dropped his hand and stepped back, his eyes resting on the candlestick nestled protectively between her breasts. "Very nice workmanship. Get it for a good price, did you?"

Sam flushed and, like a child caught with her hand in the cookie jar, whipped the candlestick behind her back. Which of course thrust her chest forward.

She raised her chin defiantly.

Chas Porter gazed down at her, his eyes slightly hooded, impossible to read.

She stared back at him. The candlestick was hers. Or was it? She felt an unexpected stab of fear. Had he seen her use her expense money to pay for it?

A young couple coming up the steps dropped hands and gave them a wide berth. "We are blocking the entrance," hissed Sam. "And, as you so rightly pointed out, I have a plane to catch."

"Not today, you don't," Chas shot back. He crooked his finger and abruptly turned away leaving her little choice but to follow him down the steps and around the side of the building.

For an instant, Sam rebelled. Who did Chas Porter think he was, calling her to task as though she were a lowly serf. He was her boss, she reassured herself as she hurried to catch up, not some feudal lord who expected her to do his bidding. Perhaps she should just tug her forelock and be done with it.

A cobblestoned alleyway separated the auction hall from its nearest neighbour, a tumbled-down ironmonger's Sam surmised from a brief glimpse at the shop window; still eking out an existence selling buckets and nails and who-knew-what.

Taking a deep breath, she plunged into the alleyway behind Chas.

It was creepy. A rickety fire escape hung from the yellowed bricks of the ironmonger's, water dripping from its bottom rung; the bolts holding it to the wall were loose and rusty with age. Sam shivered in the dank air; she could almost hear the rats scuttling in the shadows. Gripping the candlestick even tighter, she hurried to catch up to where her boss, the head of Burton-Porter & Sons, one of the country's most exclusive dealers in Fine Art & Collectibles, was waiting for her.

Her best, and perhaps only defence, Sam thought, was that she had good taste.

But then so did he. As had all the other Burtons and Porters before him. They were the ones who had taken the firm from its 18th-century beginnings as a small shop on Regent Street to the discreet upper echelons of Mayfair and Belgravia.

It probably hadn't hurt that the men in the family were all devastatingly good-looking, thought Sam, assuming the portraits lining the panelled walls in the Burton-Porter boardroom were true-to-life. Raven-haired, broad-shouldered, tall, arrogant and cold.

Just like the one waiting beneath a long-faded advertisement, its white-painted letters barely visible on the wall of the ironmonger's. Chas Porter's expression was as hard as the nails they sold. "Anything you want to say in your defence?"

Sam shook her head. "Not at the moment." She wanted to ask him if he had been the one bidding against her and, if so, why he had stopped.

Probably not a good idea.

"In my experience." He began scrubbing his chin as he spoke. "My employees generally take their extra days to fly to New York to make contacts and educate themselves by visiting galleries and showrooms…"

"Which they do at your expense…" muttered Sam.

"You're hardly in a position to say anything right now."

"I'll replace the money!"

"You're darn right you will! As for New York…"

"Oh, for heaven's sakes," Sam interrupted, "you wouldn't have hired me if I hadn't been fully qualified. And…just for the record…slinking about New York takes a lot less time than some of your staff members would have you know…"

Her voice trailed away…challenging authority was a bad habit. Once acquired, hard to lose.

"Did you know your sentences get longer when you're angry?"

Sam felt her jaw drop. "That's all you have to say!"

Chas shook his head. "Hardly." He reached into his jacket and pulled out his mobile. "Wait here. I have a couple of calls to make."

The little glimmer of fear grew and began to gnaw its way into Sam's thoughts as she watched him retreat further into the gloom. Technically speaking, she had used company funds to pay for the candlestick but surely he wouldn't…

...call the police. Or the firm's solicitors. Sam shuddered. If only she could lip read. She heard Chas say "send me a text," and then he was on to another call.

Worst case scenario, she decided, he'd fire her.

The candlestick was beginning to feel like a dead weight. The only reason she'd even known about this sale was because of a tip from a friend at a rival firm. Small sale in the Midlands, he'd said, squaring the books with Sam for a favour done in the past.

Sam had visited the auction website, which was feeble at best, read the brief description and realized that not many people would have recognized the candlestick or its history based on the information given.

So how did Chas Porter end up here?

Her head ached. With her free hand, Sam reached up and pulled the clip from her hair. As she shook it loose she felt some of the tension ease.

If Chas been able to rearrange his busy schedule to attend the sale, he must have been on the lookout for the same silver candlestick. Which meant....what?

A number of theories flitted through her brain. She needed to talk to Mia. Mia was logical. She was Sam's best friend at Burton-Porter, and she knew every piece of scuttlebutt worth knowing.

In the meantime, as far as Sam was concerned, the candlestick was hers.

She'd bought it fair and square.

And she was keeping it.

Part of him, Chas had to admit, felt a tad guilty as he covertly kept his eye on Sam. He had half-expected her to bolt but she was no coward, not by a long shot. With the sun behind her, her hair shone with copper and gold framing her face like a modern-day Madonna.

Which, he reminded himself sharply, she definitely was not.

He heard a voice in his ear and the image disappeared.

"Hello?" he said into the phone. "It's Chas.... slight change in plans."

Without revealing anything untoward about the day's events, he explained to his secretary why the assistant appraiser in the firm's art department would be going to New York instead of Samantha Redfern.

"It'll be fine. Tell her to concentrate on her own area of expertise…maybe check out the abstract expressionists while she's there. And book her into the Park Plaza. Nothing like a five-star hotel to smooth the waters."

Chas ended the call.

His focus shifted back to Sam. One problem down, another to go.

You had to admire her, thought Chas as he sauntered towards her. He knew how hard it was to stand one's ground. When he had taken control of the business, family issues had weighed heavily on his young shoulders. The company's good name was everything. He couldn't risk it then, and he wasn't going to now.

No matter how awkward the next few days might be.

Or pleasurable, he thought, as he took in the light dusting of freckles across Sam's nose and the flecks of gold in the green eyes warily tracking his approach.

"Well?" she asked. "What's the verdict?"

"The jury is still out….however, as I'm on my way to Derbyshire to catalogue an estate sale," he continued blithely. "And since you evidently know more about Georgian silver than even I realized, you will be my assistant."

"But I'm expected in New York!" Sam blustered.

He waggled his mobile in her direction. "Not anymore. Helen Chalmers will go in your stead. In fact, as I understand it, she only bowed to your persistent campaign to be the one to represent the firm because you offered to give up a day at Christmas. And yet here you are…"

"But…"

"A last minute decision, was it?"

"That is so not…" Sam sputtered.

"Fair?" Chas prompted. "As in taking it upon yourself to delay your departure to attend a sale and using your expense money to pay for a personal purchase….that kind of fair? We call it fraud here by the way…"

Sam shook her head. "I can't go…you'll have to get someone else."

"And why is that?"

A myriad of emotions crossed her face. "I have a rental car to return and, as you well know, a little banking to attend to…"

"Both of which are easily solved," countered Chas. "We can drop your car off at their office in Coventry, and grab a bite of lunch…I'm assuming you used the company account," he waited for her nod, shook his head and said, "then it's a good thing you're coming with me. You'll be able to work off your debt in no time."

"But…."

"What?" He hardened his gaze, silently daring her to take him on.

A brief flash of mutiny and then the realization dawned. She was trapped and they both knew it.

There were times, Chas reasoned as he steered her towards the high street, when one needed to spill a little ink.

In the best interest of the company, of course.

Two

Trust Chas Porter to go for the quiet elegance of a luxury car, fumed Sam, as she zoomed out of the car park in her budget rental and tucked in behind the sleek grey sedan. Almost immediately, his relentless blue eyes sought hers in the reflection of his rear view mirror. Sam tightened her grip on the steering wheel and stared straight ahead. He could check up on her all he liked. She wasn't going anywhere. Not with her luggage safely stowed, at his insistence, in the back of his car.

After fifteen minutes crawling up the high street, Sam decided a little space was in order. Easing her foot off the accelerator, she dropped back to where a delivery van had been patiently waiting for a break in the traffic. Sam flicked her lights. The driver waved his thanks and nudged into the lane ahead of her.

Effectively blocking her from Chas' view.

Score one, Samantha Redfern.

The morning had started out full of promise. After months of searching for the match to her grandmother's candlestick, she'd found it, only to have the most disturbing man she had ever met turn her life upside down.

Her eyes drifted to the passenger seat where the candlestick lay nestled in a soft scarf at the bottom of her purse. Along with her maxed-out credit card, an empty Burton-Porter envelope and the shreds of her pride.

Sam frowned. It was mortifying, the way her boss had purposefully taken over the bidding and then left her holding the bag. Yes, she'd screwed up, and yes, she would have to make up for it, but really, several days in a remote part of England when she could have been in New York City?

Think about it, the goddess of single women whispered in her ear.

You'll be stuck in an English manor house with a broad-shouldered, handsome millionaire; it's the stuff of dreams.

Sam shivered. She remembered the rock hard feel of Chas Porter's chest when she had collided with him at the auction hall, the way he'd raked her over from head to toe when she had stepped back and the sudden leap of fire in his eyes when she challenged him. For a moment, she was dazzled by the possibilities. Phooey on the goddess and her theories. Chas Porter was not a man to be trifled with. "Well, I'm not someone to be trifled with either," Sam said aloud, her voice sounding a little hollow even to her own ears. The man might be all steel and fire, but she was… determined. A survivor. Someone who knew how to win with her hard-earned smarts and dogged persistence.

What was the candlestick to him anyway? Surely, he had more than enough antique silver of his own.

A horn tapped behind her, breaking her reverie. Traffic was moving again. Sam mentally shifted gears. Her curiosity would have to wait.

The dusty van rumbled up the crest of the hill, and then swung off the main road, leaving Sam back where she'd started. Trailing sedately behind her boss, broke, indebted and indentured. Even her little black dress was being held hostage.

And there was nothing she could do about it.

Or was there?

Another large traffic circle lay ahead. They were nearing the outskirts of Coventry. Chas yielded to the traffic and signaled his intention to head northeast.

Sam moved into the slip lane behind him. His world, his rules. Angry with herself for submitting so easily, she shifted gears and sped up.

She intended to follow him, she really did, but at the last possible moment, she roared by the turn. Not indentured. Not following meekly. She went round the traffic circle a second, and a third time, putting enough distance between her and Chas Porter to flaunt her independence. He could think what he liked. She'd had a lot more riding on this trip to New York than Sotheby's, and she refused to fall into line like some recalcitrant schoolgirl.

After double-checking the map displayed on her dashboard, Sam glanced at the side mirror then deftly shifted lanes. Learning how to drive on the opposite side of the road had been a good investment, especially when it came to dealing with traffic circles. You miss your turn, you simply go around again.

Point made, Sam reached up and popped open the sun roof. The rush of cool air tousled her hair and calmed her overheated emotions. Zipping past the turnoff had been childish and she knew it, but cutting loose had made her feel better. Back in control of her own destiny, even if only for a short time. She'd spent months keeping her natural exuberance under wraps while she made her mark at Burton-Porter. No question, Chas Porter had the pedigree and the business acumen to be the star of the show. Her place was to flawlessly assess value, draw attention to overlooked treasures as antique silver collections became available, and ensure that the firm's, and his, reputation were unassailable.

Having been raised to know that reading the needs of the powerful was a survival skill, Sam carried herself accordingly – always wearing well-cut suits, the odd piece of silver jewellery, and just enough pressed powder and lipstick to feel good about herself. Not that she'd ever been one to put herself on display. Sam knew her thick, auburn hair was her best feature, but even that was kept in check. The rest of her was, well, a constant reminder not to overdo the cream cakes and double lattes.

Her stomach gurgled in response.

Sam groaned aloud. She really was hungry.

There was a pub ahead on the right, its sign swinging in the breeze. Sam eyed it longingly, but nipping in for a quick sandwich would only make things worse. Especially when the rental agency was just up the road. Even from this distance, Sam could see Chas lounging against the back of his car with his arms crossed. His stance was that of a predator biding his time, relaxed yet with muscles coiled ready to spring. Sam shivered. The dark glasses he wore made him look even more commanding…if that were possible.

If she was going to keep both the candlestick and her job, she would have to act as though she were in the showrooms at Burton-Porter dealing with a well-heeled client, instead of raging against the ruggedly handsome man now orchestrating her every move.

At least, he was easy on the eye. With disquieting warmth, Sam remembered how she had felt when he had briefly held and steadied her. In that instant she had felt safe. No man had ever made her feel that way before.

Sam braced herself for whatever was to come and turned into the parking lot.

Carefully nosing into a vacant space, she cut the ignition and set the handbrake. She grabbed her shoulder bag with its precious cargo off the passenger seat and slipped out of the car.

"Waiting long?" she asked Chas politely.

The dark glasses swung her way. "Long enough to settle your account."

"Just add it to my tab," said Sam archly. She began walking towards the small building which housed the offices of the rental car agency.

"Where do you think you're going?" barked Chas.

Without breaking her stride, Sam stretched out her arm and jangled the car keys.

"I told you I'd already settled the account."

Sam spun around to face him. "Don't they have to check the car for damages?" she asked, forcing herself to smile sweetly.

"Not if they want our business." They glared at each other across the tarmac, but the expression on Chas Porter's face brooked no protest.

"Fine," said Sam. Chin up, she strolled back to the rental car, tossed the keys inside, and then paused to draw a calming breath. If that's the way he wanted to play it, she decided silently, then that's the way it would be. She'd pushed her luck enough for the moment.

"Now that that's done, I suggest we stop for a bite to eat."

"Fine," Sam repeated. At least she wouldn't suffer the embarrassment of a rumbling stomach in his lordship's company.

Sam gave him a wide berth and strode up the side of the sedan, half-expecting him to open the door for her. Obviously, he was not as gallant as she'd thought. He hadn't budged.

A deep chuckle reached Sam as soon as her hand closed around the door handle.

"Planning on driving my car as well, were you?"

Face burning, Sam snatched her hand away. Nearly two years in England, a brand new British drivers' licence, and in her seething fury, she'd forgotten which side of the car she was supposed to be on.

"My apologies," drawled Chas as she marched past his grinning face to the passenger side. "I thought you had purposely driven around the roundabout an extra time or two just to spite me… but it turns out you really don't know where you're going, do you?"

She'd behaved like a fool, thought Sam.

And they both knew it.

Thirty-love, Chas Porter.

By the time they arrived at the elegant inn he had chosen for lunch, Chas found himself more than a tad irritated. Not only had this new version of Miss Redfern barely spoken during the twenty minutes it had taken them to reach their destination, she had slipped out of the car the second they got there. Without waiting for him to reach her door. His scowl softened as he watched her approach the inn's weathered steps and then pause as if suddenly unsure. Caught by the way the sunlight burnished her hair with flares of red and gold, Chas felt his body tense. He had to force down the enticing image of what it would feel like to wind his fingers in the soft curls and pull her into his grasp. She turned to him then, one eyebrow arched enquiringly and he felt the heat crackle between them. The soft skin at the base of her throat took on a blush that rose to her face, highlighting the creaminess of her flawless complexion and the emerald green of her eyes.

Hiding the pressing surge of awareness, Chas gestured toward the door and said gruffly, "Shall we go in?"

Sam nodded and went ahead, hesitating for a moment at the entrance when the formally clad maître d' came forward to greet them

The only sign she gave that this wasn't an everyday lunch was the telltale up tilt of her chin as they were ushered past elegant arrangements of orchids to a table set with pristine linens and gleaming silverware. She smiled pleasantly and took her seat, barely moving until the waiter had poured their ice water.

Bemused and somewhat wary to find his firm's ever-so-cool silver appraiser was as prickly as a hedgehog, Chas kept his eye on Sam as she drained the last of her water. When she'd let out a satisfied sigh, he asked. "And are you hungry as well?"

"Starving."

She exchanged her empty glass for a menu, blithely holding it in front of her face so that it shielded her from view. "You?" she asked.

"Famished," replied Chas. Miss Redfern was definitely turning into a rather unexpected personality. She had flouted his orders in every possible way short of outright rebellion and he was not entirely sure he liked it. His work required focus and held no place, personally or professionally, for a woman who zigged and zagged. He wanted the women in his personal life to sparkle with elegance and charm without ever outstaying their welcome. Professionally, he wanted his employees to act like…well, like Samantha Redfern had until the candlestick had come into her possession. Chas' lips tightened. He had no intention of encouraging Miss Redfern's sudden show of independence. Yet how to explain this insane desire to take her under his wing?

"Their steak and kidney pie is excellent," he informed the top of her head. "And it comes with a salad."

"Thank you." Sam lowered her menu, snapped it shut and set it to one side, carefully aligning its spine with the edge of the linen tablecloth.

In spite of his determination to regard her as just another employee, Chas noticed that her fingers were long and tapered. She wore no rings, just a slim silver bracelet on her right arm, wristwatch on her left.

He signalled the waiter. "Red wine?"

"I could use a drink," Sam admitted.

Chas quickly scanned the wine list. "Bad day?"

"Umm, I'd say 'mixed', at best."

Amused, Chas quickly placed their order and then leaned back in his chair, unabashedly studying Sam as she discreetly took in the restaurant's opulent surroundings.

Had she grown up in England, her accent, her schooling and her connections, often an important part of their business, would have told him everything he needed to know about her. Perhaps he didn't know his staff as well as he thought. An oversight he was determined to rectify. Beginning now.

"So," he said, "Miss Redfern."

Her green eyes drifted back to his. "Mr. Porter."

"Lest we sit here like a long-married couple who have lost the ability to converse, try telling me something about you I don't know."

Her left brow rose in a perfect arch. "Like what?"

"Like why you would bid way beyond your pay grade to buy one silver candlestick?"

He'd meant to be flip but as soon as the words were out of his mouth, Chas realized his earlier fury was still close to the surface. He considered apologizing, but Sam cut him off.

"You, sir," she hissed across the table, "have a lot of...."

"What?" Chas shot back. "Leverage?"

"Actually, what I was going to say was...." she stopped abruptly.

Their waiter was hovering a few feet away with their wine.

Chas waved him forward. The young man presented the bottle to Chas, then deftly removed its cork and poured a small amount in Chas' wine glass.

Casually swirling the ruby red liquid about the bowl of his glass, Chas tried not to think about Sam glaring at him from the other side of the table. She knew he'd watched her take a shawl from her suitcase and wrap it around the candlestick. She knew he suspected it was now in that oversized bag of hers resting on the floor next to her chair. But what she didn't know was how much he was enjoying every second he spent in her company.

Raising his glass, he breathed in the wine's burgundian bouquet. It was superb. He took an appreciative sip and with a nod to the waiter, their glasses were filled.

"Is there anything we might drink to without getting into a fight?" he asked Sam as the young man withdrew.

"How about my impeccable taste in silver," suggested Sam raising her glass in mock salute.

She touched the glass to her lips and took a slow sip, letting it linger as she savoured its bouquet. "This is delicious."

"I'm glad you like it…" Chas sat quietly with his wine and waited.

And then Sam began to speak. "I saw a painting when I was a young girl…called Five O'Clock Tea. It was only a picture in a book… about women silversmiths," she blushed slightly.

"Two young Victorian women sitting on a chintz sofa. There's a silver tea service arranged on the table in front of them. One wears a hat and gloves and sips from a delicate porcelain cup. She's the visitor. They're just friends having tea, yet it was so…captivating."

Enchanted, Chas watched the memories play across Sam's face. She really was beautiful, and so much more real to him than she had ever been before.

She must have sensed he was looking at her. "I guess I was hooked."

"On silver?" asked Chas.

Sam laughed. "Tea parties. My grandmother was a good sport."

Suddenly, Chas found he couldn't take his eyes off her. Their gazes caught across the table, the one waiting for the other. Then the jagged ring of a mobile phone stole the moment.

Chas sighed. "Yours?"

Flushing, Sam groped beneath the table. "Mine." She popped back up with the offending device in her hand.

Her forehead scrunched as she scanned the display screen.

It was a text. And judging by the sudden flash of anger in those gorgeous green eyes, the word was out at Burton-Porter.

Sam turned off her phone and put it away. What on earth was she thinking?

Nattering on like that to a boss who was, without doubt, one of the most self-assured men she had ever met. Not to mention rich and well-educated, handsome, stylish…and, up until today, perfectly boring. She raised her glass.

He probably had his own sommelier at boarding school, she thought crossly.

"I started in the wine department," said Chas as though he'd read her mind. He continued to gently swirl the wine about his glass with perfect ease. "Probably because I was young enough to shift the crates and scared enough to be careful. The boss's son is not always the most popular person on staff…people tend to resent you…" he smiled ruefully, "and leap to conclusions."

"Hardly surprising."

"Hey! I only broke one bottle. Unfortunately, it was a hundred-year-old claret. Very expensive."

"Oops," Sam sympathized.

"My father was less than amused…"

There's a story there, thought Sam as a shadow flickered across his brow. She'd heard rumours, of course, but nothing out of the norm. Parents divorced, near financial ruin, and then according to one of the firm's most rabid gossips, along came Chas. And all was well.

"Your turn," prompted Chas.

"I'm sorry?"

"I've done my fair share of filling in the awkward moments. Tell me something about yourself I don't know." Chas set his glass down and leaned forward, his left elbow on the table, his chin cupped in the palm of his hand. "Like why you have such a problem with authority?"

"How about because you're rich and I'm not."

"I don't buy it. You work well with everyone. In fact, the silver department has benefited enormously from your expertise. Try again."

Neither his expression nor his oh-so-ever blue eyes revealed anything but a polite interest. Sam cleared the flutter from her throat. That her parents had been killed in an accident when she was a baby was none of Chas Porter's business.

"So what about you?" she asked sweetly, "Any other bullies in your family, or are you the only one?"

She'd tried to deflect the conversation, but all she'd done was hurt him. His fingers curled about the stem of his wine glass and he sat twisting it from side to side then he turned to gaze through the leaded panes of the restaurant's window.

Sam sucked in a quiet breath. The old inn was an oasis of privilege, elegant place settings and soft music, well-dressed people enjoying a late lunch and quiet conversation.

She felt Chas' eyes return to scrutinize her. The light had gone out of them; they were flat like the pre-storm stillness of the great lakes. "Is that how you see me?" he asked quietly. "Nothing more than a bully in a suit?"

Sam shook her head. "No...not at all. I really don't know where that came from...I..."

She felt small and ungracious. The man had given her an opportunity to make amends for her flagrant misuse of company funds and all she could do was poke at him like a picador jabbing a bull.

The waiter appeared with their lunch. Sam murmured her thanks and then busied herself with her salad. It was a piquant mix of mustard greens and sun-dried tomatoes; and the steak and kidney pie was delicious. "You were right," she ventured after a few minutes. "The steak and kidney pie was an excellent choice."

"Glad you like it."

They ate in silence like the long-married couple Chas so obviously never wanted to be part of. Sam sighed. It was better than trying to undo the damage she'd already done. And besides, what did she know about marriage anyway? Or love, for that matter. Other than a burning need that never went away, and an embarrassing tendency to tear up whenever she heard a sappy song on the radio, Sam had always stayed clear of entanglement. It was safer that way.

"Penny?" said Chas.

Sam bristled beneath his gaze. "No."

"All right then. Do you ride?" he asked.

"Horses?" she asked, interest flaring.

"That is what I had in mind."

"I haven't been on a horse since I was twelve years old."

"Pony club?"

"Hardly." It had been at the Toronto race course where her grandfather had worked, but that would require another explanation she wasn't going to share.

"Besides, I have nothing to wear…" Sam said with an almost imperceptible flick of her fork towards their fellow diners, older well-dressed women for the most part, a few couples, and scattered about the room, several tables for four taken up with men and women in expensive suits. "I mean, really, do I look like I belong here?"

"Actually, yes." Chas mouth twitched. "I'm sure Mrs. Weekes will be able to find something suitable," he said sizing her up with a practised eye. "Unless of course, you'd rather ride side saddle in one of the little black dresses you were undoubtedly taking to New York."

Sam's eyes twinkled. "Life was easier when you were simply Chas 'bloody' Porter."

"Not well-liked, then."

"Let's just say you are well-respected."

"I suppose that's something…" he mused. When Sam didn't respond, he went back to his lunch.

If she could just get through the next few days, Sam decided as she polished off the last of her wine, she would be fine. Older and wiser. And fine.

"At least, I know you like the burgundy. And

no," Chas held up his hands, "that was not intended as a cheap shot." He reached for the near-empty bottle. "More?"

Samantha felt her face redden. "No, thank you."

"Good call." He checked his watch. "It's gone three. There is no rush but I would prefer to be there by dark."

"And where exactly is there?"

"The Peak District."

"We're going to the Peak District!"

Chas cocked his head. "Problem?"

Sam shook hers. "No, no. It's just…I don't know…" She dabbed the corners of her mouth with her napkin. "A long way away."

If Chas was puzzled by her reaction, he hid it well, droning on about estates and how difficult it could be to catalogue them for sale. "Only to have them change their minds," she heard him say, "plays havoc with my schedule." He shrugged. "Occupational hazard, I guess."

"And today's auction?" she asked, "Was that mere happenstance or were you searching for something in particular?" Not that she thought her employer did anything spontaneous. "You can imagine my surprise…." she continued, "…one minute I'm the lone bidder and the next I'm watching my bank account and my career go down the drain. And just to add insult to injury, you drop out of the bidding. Why was that?"

"Because the game was wearing thin."

"Oh." If only she could go back to her flat in London, unpack and pretend today never happened. Everything would be fine.

But then Chas tossed his own napkin on the table, and leaned in close. The heady mix of his distinctive scent was hers for the taking. And she did, inhaling deeply. "What would you say," he said in an undertone, "if I told you I was at the auction hall today because I wanted to spend more time with you?"

"I'd call you a liar," she said sweetly hoping her voice didn't betray the quiver in her belly.

"And you'd be...partially right." He drew back, a sardonic grin on his face. "Nonetheless. You are stuck with me for the next few days. So let's drop the Mr. Porter. I'll be Chas and you'll be what... Sam or Samantha...which do you prefer by the way?"

"Sam."

Chas stuck out his hand. "Chas."

Nodding as much to herself as to the man across the table, Sam placed her right hand in his.

And instantly realized her mistake.

His eyes might be shot with steel, but his skin radiated warmth. And strength. Her breath caught as his hand closed around hers...it felt so good, she couldn't hide the shiver of pleasure rippling its way through her body.

And then she remembered. This was her boss, the man to whom she was seriously indebted. She tugged her hand from his grasp, grabbed her bag and pushed back her chair.

"I have to go," she stammered. "To the toilets."

She took one look at the knowing grin on his face and bolted for the door.

Outside the dining room, everything was quiet. Relieved, Sam hurried along the plush carpet of the hallway, past the reception desk and down the corridor to the ladies'.

She really was bursting for a pee. And a little privacy because this, she fumed as she locked the cubicle door behind her, was probably her last chance for either.

It would take several hours to get there, Chas had said before he decided they should break for lunch. Still, Sam was glad they'd stopped. She'd had no time to eat before the auction and now her stomach felt uncomfortable after the rich food and wine.

Her jeans seemed to have shrunk accordingly.

She gave them a final tug, then gathered her belongings and headed for the sink. She would have to watch her step. In two short hours, Chas Porter had managed to finesse more information out of her than anyone else she'd met since she had arrived in England.

While in exchange she had learned virtually nothing.

Or had she? A definite chink had appeared in his armour when she'd quizzed him about his family. Perhaps he wasn't as cold as he let on. Sam peered into the mirror. She'd certainly detected a touch of warmth when he'd held her hand…

Enough already, Sam scolded herself. She had the candlestick, now all she had to do was wiggle her way out of her current dilemma.

She delved into her bag for her mobile phone.

It rang as soon as she switched it on.

"Hey, Mia."

"Don't 'hey' me! Where are you? And why didn't you answer my text?"

"I'm in Coventry," drawled Sam wrinkling her nose at her own reflection.

"Where?"

"Coventry. It's in Warwickshire, I'm told."

"Whatever. You should see this place…there hasn't been this much action since Nigel smashed that vase." It was easy to picture Mia, headset on, arms flapping dramatically as she described the scene at Burton-Porter & Sons.

Sam ran a finger over her eyebrow.

"…your replacement tore out of here an hour ago looking like she'd just won the Grand National! And Chas' secretary had to close her door. She never does that."

"Whoa, slow down," said Sam. It was worse than she thought. "Please tell her I am really, really sorry about the upset."

"This is so not in my job description," Mia muttered. "Where are you exactly? You are still in England, yeah?"

"Actually, I am in a very posh toilet…hang on…"

She could hear male voices in the corridor. One of which sounded exactly like Chas. Unfortunately, she couldn't make out what they were saying. The conversation stopped, footsteps resumed and she heard the pneumatic sound of a heavy door closing.

Sam retreated into the cubicle and locked the door.

"Talk louder…"

"I can't," hissed Sam. "There is one thin wall between me and you-know-who and I can't afford any more issues."

"So it's true…you really did blow off New York…"

And possibly my career, thought Sam. "…there was this country auction…unfortunately; I wasn't the only one from Burton-Porter in the audience."

"Whoa! Then the rumours are true…"

"What rumours?" Sam scrubbed her forehead. It was full of creases which would turn into wrinkles. Next thing she knew she would be prematurely grey. Anxiety did that to a person.

"The word is you've gone rogue otherwise you would have never have gone to an auction when you're supposed to be in New York and everyone thinks you're playing the boss cause you want a pay rise."

"That is so not true." Sam's cheeks burned at the thought.

"Ah, well. Don't worry about that," continued Mia. "The smart money is on you and Chas having a romantic getaway somewhere in the wilds of Scotland."

Sam rested her forehead against the wall of the cubicle.

"While it is true that *Mister* Porter and I did bump into each other at an auction," she froze… there was a rat-a-tap-tap on the outside door. Had to be Chas. Sam covered the phone. "Go away!" she shouted.

"And given," she continued her conversation with Mia through clenched teeth, "that we were already halfway to Derbyshire, *Mister* Porter suggested that I help him catalogue an estate in the Peak District."

"Regardless," said Mia stiffly. "It would have been nice if you'd told your friends what you were up to…we thought you were already in New York."

"Look, Mia. I am sorry but it all happened so fast."

"Y'uh, huh. A guy I could understand…but an auction…" Mia's voice trailed away and Sam knew she was thinking about the young man she'd met at a club a few weeks back.

"I'll explain it all when I see you?"

"Full disclosure?"

Sam hesitated.

Whatever did, or did not, happen between her and Chas Porter was no one's business but theirs. And as his behaviour had been so totally in keeping with his image at the office of a cold, arrogant man, to-the-manor-born and don't you forget it kind of guy, there would be nothing to tell. So why was she all tied up in knots?

Sam sighed. Mia was her closest friend at Burton-Porter. She'd even invited Sam to go home with her the previous Christmas. A kindness Sam would never forget.

"Deal." Sam replied, "Only you don't tell anyone I called….no matter what. But see if you can find out anything about a big estate coming on the market. Name of Weekes. The boss is a little vague on the details."

"The man's such a control freak."

"That's a whole other issue." All of a sudden, Sam felt herself itching to join the man waiting for her in the car. Perhaps spending time in a remote part of England wasn't such a bad idea after all.

"Mia…"

"Yeees?"

"Repeat after me…this is strictly business, right?"

"Absolutely," Mia replied. "If anybody asks, I'll tell them you are on a strictly-business trip. With *Mister strictly-business* Chas Porter."

"Don't you dare! Mia!"

But all Sam got back was raucous laughter.

Three

"You are not going to be sick, are you?"

Sam curled her fingers around the edge of the passenger seat and forced a smile. Now was not the time to betray *any* weakness to her boss. "No of course not." She swallowed hard. "Shouldn't have had all that steak and kidney pie."

Not to mention the wine. Or most of all, the emotional rollercoaster of the last few hours spent with a man like Chas Porter. The rich smell of fine leather mingled with the fresh scent of the clean, virile male beside her threatened to overwhelm her senses as much as the overly rich meal had overwhelmed her stomach.

Seeking relief, Sam pressed the side of her face against the cool glass of the passenger window as they zipped along on the B64-something-or-other. They were near Bakewell, or was it Buxton? She'd lost track. She caught a flash of blue in an otherwise blurry landscape as they raced beneath a giant railway trestle and then rose from the gorge as though they were shooting the rapids. A controlled flick of his wrist and Chas steered the car around a curve, breaking away from the cleft valley into the heart of the Peak District.

Here, the scene was more familiarly pastoral. Sheep dotted the hillsides. Endless miles of dry stone walls delineated the boundaries of every field and holding as far as the eye could see. A few trees punctuated the landscape, and in the far distance, she could see a man striding across the acres with a pair of dogs bounding ahead of him. Sam had a sudden picture of Chas and Chas' ancestors doing just that, the lords of all they surveyed, walking their land. The upper-crust reserve he displayed in London had its roots in a place like this, Sam mused. Perhaps hers lay in similar ground. As her eyes strayed across Chas' high cheekbones and determined jaw, testimony to generations of breeding, she let out a soft, involuntary sigh and forced herself to look back at the scenery.

It was, Sam decided, ruggedly beautiful. And a welcome change from worrying about how she was going to spend several days in close proximity with a man who had half the female staff at Burton-Porter tracking him like hunter/warriors whenever he entered a room. Didn't they realize how dangerous it was to hunt the hunter?

"You've gone silent on me again." Chas interrupted her thoughts.

"I've been busy watching my life flash before my eyes."

"You're lucky it's not the weekend." Chas deftly geared down for another hairpin turn. "You would not believe the number of motorcyclists through here on a Sunday…even I find it unnerving."

"Good to know," muttered Sam. She didn't care anymore. "These roads just get smaller and smaller." Sam lowered her window all the way and laughed. "Driving in England is not for the faint of heart," she called. "The criminally insane maybe…"

She was rewarded with the same deep chuckle she'd heard earlier.

"You have a nice laugh," she shouted over the rush of the wind.

He smiled back at her and she realized what an amazingly attractive man he was. As their eyes met, the air in the car sizzled. Sam felt the tingle deep in her being as his hot gaze dove into her soul.

She was lost and then she caught sight of the curve ahead.

Suddenly, it was upon them. A Land Rover barrelled directly towards the car, its massive grill bearing down on them at top speed. Sam let out a piercing scream and grabbed for the dash.

Chas' head whipped around. Startled, he hesitated. Barely a fraction of a second, but it was enough. The sickening screech of metal rubbing on metal as the driver of the Land Rover jerked his wheel. At the very last second a break appeared in the wall, and Chas yanked the car into the space.

He hammered the steering wheel with the flat of his hand as the Land Rover sped away.

Chas switched off the engine. Silence. They sat staring straight ahead, Sam burning with humiliation. She stole a glance at Chas' profile. An angry muscle worked in the corner of his cheek.

"There seems to be no end to your talents, Miss Redfern," seethed Chas, his voice barely in check. His stormy eyes swung toward her. Sam felt herself shrinking into the seat.

"I thought he was going to hit us," she muttered.

"And thanks to your interference, he did." Chas flung open his door and went to inspect the damage.

Sam froze. Tears of indignation rose to her eyes. Despondent, she dashed them away. One minute, they were on the verge of something special and in a nanosecond it had vanished and she was left with Chas "bloody" Porter again. "What does he expect?" she muttered furiously to herself. "Driving like a maniac."

She scrambled out through the driver's side to inspect the damage for herself and gasped. It was awful. Paint was skinned from the front all the way to the rear bumper. The back door was creased, and the fender had a distinct tilt that had not been there before.

Chas ran his fingers lovingly along the car's ruined finish, felt the dent in the door, and then pushed on the bumper in a vain attempt to straighten it.

"I'm sorry," Sam said in a small voice. When he didn't even look at her, let alone answer, her apology gave way to anger. "Of course if you hadn't been driving like a crazy person, this wouldn't have happened."

He looked at her then, a long icy stare of rage and contempt. Sam stiffened.

"What?" Chas thundered. "Your ill-timed shriek like your ill-timed foray into your own plans this morning is a pattern for disaster! And you accept no responsibility?"

"That's not what I meant!" Sam jammed her hands into her hips, in full battle mode. "You were driving too fast for a narrow road like this. And you should take responsibility for your actions instead of blaming your minions."

"I'll have you know, Miss Redfern, that I have driven this road a thousand times and this is the one and only time my passenger's hysterical screams caused me to have an accident."

"Then your passengers were blind idiots," Sam raged. "I didn't scream for the fun of it! It was a simple reaction to death coming straight for me! Which your driving caused!"

"And I suppose it's my fault you delayed your trip to New York to do a little business on the side, and pay for it with company funds?" Chas snapped back. He swung his arm towards his damaged car. "And shall I add this to your tab as well, Miss Redfern?" he added mockingly. "You are a rather expensive employee, and while you are definitely not a minion, the question is…are you worth the trouble?"

Sam glared at him mutely, spun on her heel and crawled back into the passenger side of the car. Slouching down in her seat, Sam ran through a dozen scenarios when her boss would be brought to his knees and beg for her help. And she would walk away laughing. Hah!

But when Chas at last got into the car and silently turned the ignitions key, her rage drained away into despair. Maybe it was a little her fault for shrieking. But only a little. He shouldn't drive like he owned the road, like he was better and stronger and more accomplished than everyone else in his vicinity.

Same stole a glance at his uncompromising profile. Despite herself, she could not help admiring the strength of his grasp on the wheel, the way he handled the high-speed automobile. How oddly challenging it was having a boss who looked as though he would be at home on the page of a high-end magazine advertising Tag watches or Burberry weekend wear. His dark hair was just long enough to curl over his collar and the few strands of grey at his temple emphasized the controlled strength he radiated. The accident had not caused him to reduce his speed, Sam noted. If anything he was driving faster.

Chas eased up on the accelerator as they approached a small village; little more than a cluster of cottages really. Ahead, Sam could see an old man, bent and weathered, steadfastly herding a flock of sheep across the road in front of them.

Chas slowed to a crawl and lowered his window.

As they drew nearer, the farmer raised his fingers to his cap.

A pungent combination of damp earth and barnyard wafted through the open windows. Chas stuck his head out as they crept past the hindquarters of a particularly large-bottomed ewe. The old man stood by the gate urging the stragglers with his stick. A black-and-white border collier ran alongside, nipping at the heels of any sheep who thought to stray.

"Evening, George," said Chas.

The old farmer eyed the ragged damage to the car but made no comment. "And here I was thinking you were too good for the likes of us."

Sam gave an almost inaudible snort. Chas gave no sign of hearing beyond a slight tightening of his hands on the wheel. "London keeps me busy."

"You'll need a better excuse than that, lad. Evelyn Weekes is beginning to fret."

"I suspect her angst has more to do with her husband."

"Aye. Still, John's better than nought."

"It's hard work being an estate manager these days," retorted Chas. He shoved the car back into gear and began to inch his way past the old man. They exchanged another nod. George tipped his hat to Sam. She raised her hand to wave but the moment was lost.

Twisting in her seat, she watched him through the rear window as he grew smaller and smaller and then faded from sight.

"Who was that?" she asked turning back round.

"A former tenant...estate worker."

"How quaint."

"Don't go there," growled Chas.

Sam opened her mouth to protest but thought better of it. There was something here she wasn't picking up on, but for the life of her, she had no idea what it was.

And when they crested the ridge a few minutes later, she forgot all about it.

The evening sun had burst through the clouds, bathing the valley which lay before them in layers of red and orange and neon pink. All thoughts of the dreadful day vanished in the ineffable magnificence blending man's work and nature before her.

"It's so beautiful," breathed Sam.

Despite the fact that his pulse was racing and his teeth were clenching of their own accord, Chas felt himself relax a little at Samantha's words. He *had* been driving too fast earlier, determined not to give in to his reluctance to face all the memories which permeated the walls of the great house before them. And somehow, he was even more sure now that Sam's buoyant spirit would be the shield he needed against the ghosts of his past.

Stretching the truth, he had done, but everything was going to be fine.

Besides, with her expertise and experience, it shouldn't take more than a week to get the massive job of cataloguing everything from books to portraits to porcelain underway. The detritus of generations past.

He risked another glance at the woman beside him as they entered the gates of Burton Park. She rewarded him with a luminous smile, her eyes sparkling with pleasure. Even the setting sun was on her side, spinning her hair into strands of copper and gold as they flitted in and out of the rippling shadows along the oak-lined drive.

The house had long since been swept clean of the wrangling demands of his father's last girlfriend and his mother's reappearance and demands for more money. It had been three months since he'd been here. And even then he had only stayed a couple of nights despite Mrs. Weekes' roast lamb and the promise of curry to come.

Story of his life.

Just popped in to collect my hiking gear, he would say, kissing Mrs. Weekes on the cheek and vowing to return very, very soon. For her. Never for his family, such as it was.

He hadn't intended to come today, but Sam's courage in the face of the candlestick disaster had prodded him to see how he could face the demons of his past and the practicalities of his inheritance. And if she could stand there with her chin up, like David taunting Goliath, he could certainly do the same.

He was very glad of Sam's company even if he had forced it upon her in a most unusual way. She hadn't been kidnapped, he told himself with a twinge of guilt, simply redeployed. And of course, he had been amply repaid for his misdeeds by the ruin of his car. Yet as they emerged from the trees, and the wide expanse of parkland unfolded before them, he knew that whatever lay ahead of him, he wouldn't regret it.

"What is this place?" breathed Sam.

"Wait. Just another minute or two."

He drew up in front of the manor house and shut off the ignition.

They sat in silence, listening to the metallic tick of the engine as it settled and cooled. For a moment Chas watched Sam's wide eyes dance over the beauty of the old house. Then as the comfortable silence continued, he turned his attention from her to the manor. The copper gutters on the far wing of the stable needed tending, Chas noted. Last autumn's leaves had gathered in the corners, left to form small pyramids of brown and russet compost.

His estate manager was getting older, still trying to do everything single-handedly, and not quite achieving it.

Yet another in a long list of issues Chas knew he must resolve.

He fought against the echoes in his head that plagued him every time he returned; the shouting, the recriminations, the furious arguments as his parents' marriage disintegrated into a slogging match of who did what to whom. Boarding school had been a sanctuary. And then there was peace, peace cloaked in desolation for him when his mother had left and started another family without him.

He had to tell Sam the truth and he had to tell her quickly, before the tide of bitter emotion washed over him. "Welcome to Porter Hall," he said softly.

Sam stiffened in the seat beside him.

"Porter Hall…" she whispered.

Chas could almost feel her turning it over in her mind. "I don't understand. You said we were going to catalogue an estate sale." Her eyes flashed her anger.

"We are," snapped Chas, "And while we're at it, you are going to work off your debt to Burton-Porter."

"But Porter Hall is your home, isn't it?"

"It is."

"And Mrs. Weekes?" Sam demanded. "What about her?"

"My housekeeper." Chas yanked on the hand brake. "But you needn't worry. We'll be well-chaperoned. The Weekes have a flat above the coach house."

But Sam was having none of it. "What kind of game are you playing at?" Her voice was steady but the accusation was loud and clear.

He was the worst kind of lowlife.

Just another in a long line of Burton-Porter males who manipulated everyone around them.

Sam reached for the door handle.

Chas grabbed her other arm. "Wait." His heart was hammering in his chest. "Let me explain."

"No. You wait," she hissed, spitting the words at him as though they left a bad taste in her mouth. "You used your position to take advantage of me. You purposely misled me. And now you're holding me against my will."

She wrenched her arm from his grasp and kicked open the door with the heel of her boot. "And to think you were threatening me with fraud," she shouted back. "You will *not* get away with this."

Chas felt the blood drain from his face. Just like his father and grandfather had done so often, he had tricked a woman into doing what he wanted. How on earth could he have been such a fool?

If Evelyn Weekes had been put out by their unexpected arrival, she hid it well. Taking one covert look at Sam's flaming face and Chas' set expression, she sidestepped what could have been an extremely awkward moment by herding them through the flagstone entrance way and into the grand hall, all with brisk murmurs of pleasure at seeing Chas back in his home.

"This is my colleague, Miss Redfern," said Chas stiffly. He lowered the larger of Sam's two cases to the floor. "She'll be staying a few days. Helping me catalogue the antiques and silver."

Mrs. Weekes seemed to take it in stride. "Your room is ready for you. I'll see to Miss Redfern."

"Thank you, Mrs. Weekes," Chas said. "If your husband is about, I'd like to have a quick word with him. Hopefully, he can recommend a good body shop in the area." Ignoring Sam, Chas nodded to Mrs. Weekes, and then headed toward the back of his house.

"This way, please." The housekeeper picked up the suitcase Chas had carried in from the car and started up the broad staircase toward the galleried upper floor.

Sam sighed. What choice did she have? She could hardly run after Chas and demand to be taken to a hotel, even if there was one anywhere within miles. Resigned, she hefted her second bag and followed the sturdy figure up the stone stairs.

The landing was large and foreboding with dimly-lit corridors heading off in three directions. "Shades of Jane Eyre," Sam muttered, but smiled brightly when Mrs. Weekes eyebrows arched.

"The main part of the house was built in the late eighteenth century by William Porter," the housekeeper said. "He made a fortune as one of the new agriculturalists. But by the time, Reginald Porter, Chas' grandfather came along, the estate had fallen on hard times. That's when he married Eugenie Burton, Chas' grandmother."

"The Burtons were in the East India trade, weren't they?" That was all Sam knew; the Burton-Porter website contained a very short and carefully-worded family history.

"The Burtons were always well-travelled," said Mrs. Weekes. "But the Porters had the lineage. This way." Her stiff manner relaxed as they walked the corridor. She pointed out a small study by Constable which begged for better lighting; there were several fine Victorian pastorals and a few mediocre portraits but it was the exquisite porcelain vase on a nearby table which caught Sam in its thrall. She gently touched its magnificent finish. It was as exciting as being in any of the New York showrooms. Speaking of which, she wondered what on earth was being said back at the London office.

"There were a great many treasures in this house," continued Mrs. Weekes. "The family always appreciated beautiful things and enjoyed a large circle of friends. When I first came to work at Porter Hall," she went on, "the housekeeper, that would have been Mrs. Betts if memory serves, always said a grand house should keep a guest room ready at all times. One never knows when the family will arrive…"

"…or with whom," muttered Sam.

"Precisely. And which are you, Miss Redfern?" A twinkle in the housekeeper's brown eyes softened the enquiry. "Colleague, paramour, or third-cousin twice-removed?"

"Now that's a scary thought," laughed Sam. "Better put me down as an employee who, by rights, should have been halfway across the Atlantic by now. Our boss shanghaied me this morning to help catalogue the collections."

Mrs. Weekes stopped at the next doorway. "In that case, I suspect you've had a long day…You do seem a bit pale. Are you all right?"

Sam frowned. What should she say? That the day had been one long series of disasters and that she and Chas had sparred like children? Or should she mention that she had used company funds to buy herself a silver candlestick?

"I'm fine, thank you. I just need a good cup of tea."

"Then why don't you settle in while I nip downstairs and fetch you a pot of tea and something to tide you over." Mrs. Weekes reached for the door handle. The door swung inwards. Sam followed the housekeeper inside. "Will this suit you, then, Miss Redfern?" she asked placing Sam's bag at the foot of the bed.

"Oh, lovely," Sam breathed as her gaze swept over the elegant four-poster bed, the Edwardian dressing table and chair, and on to the armoire glowing richly in the soft light from the nightstand. There was even a window seat with a bevy of soft pillows all done up in dusty rose and sage to match the window's voluminous curtains.

"Compared to my flat in London, Mrs. Weekes, this is the height of luxury."

Pleased by the compliment, the housekeeper crossed over to the window and drew back the curtains. "I'll just let in a bit of air, shall I?" With a practised hand, she released the catch on the casement and nudged open the window. Give it a minute or two," she advised, "and you'll think the room was done up fresh."

Sam slipped her heavy purse off her shoulder and set her suitcase on the floor. "Um…the bathroom is?"

"Over there, dear." The housekeeper pointed to a white panelled door on the far wall next to which sat an inviting chintz-covered wing chair in the same peony and rose pattern as the drapes.

She paused to worry a wrinkle out of the bed covers. "I often set out a plate of sandwiches in the dining room when we have late arrivals," she said massaging the small of her back as she straightened. "Down the stairs, turn right, second door on the left."

"Thank you, Mrs. Weekes. I'll be fine." said Sam.

As soon as the housekeeper was out the door, Sam headed for the sanctuary of the window seat. She tugged off her boots and dropped them to the floor. At least, her toes were happy. What a day. She was tempted to flop back against the cushions and just lie there but first…she had to call Mia. How had she been so stupid as to tell her friend anything at all in their earlier conversation? Discretion not being Mia's strong suit, the last thing Sam wanted was to have everyone in the office scratching their heads over an estate sale that didn't exist. Sooner or later, someone would link Mrs. Weekes to Porter Hall and the whole sordid story would be revealed.

But when Sam switched on her mobile, she had no reception. She held it up to the window and watched the little icon search the heavens in vain.

Porter Hall was in a dead zone. No service. No contact. And nowhere to go.

Four

Chas swirled the aged single malt in his glass and uttered a soft string of curses. Life wasn't fair and, quite frankly, it was often ill-timed. Before today, his relationship with Samantha Redfern had been cool and professional and, he liked to think, based on mutual respect.

Not anymore.

During the course of a single day, he'd admired her moxie, lost his temper and been utterly intrigued by her. And now he couldn't decide whether he was totally enamoured with her or just plain furious.

Probably a bit of both.

In an effort to banish the picture of her flashing eyes and defiant chin, Chas began to mentally catalogue her crimes of the day.

She had stolen the candlestick using money from the firm he owned, created a potentially embarrassing furor at his company, and most heinous of all, caused the wreck of his car. Chas tried to whip himself into a satisfying rage at Ms. Redfern, but the image of her standing there, clutching the silver candlestick and fighting to the last ditch even though they both knew she was in the wrong, kept intruding into his mind. Giving up, he tried to focus on the damage done to the side of his car, but there she was again with sunlight shimmering over her auburn hair as she insisted that being sideswiped by the Land Rover was *his* fault, not hers.

He didn't know whether to laugh or go strangle her, which she so obviously deserved. Unfortunately, no matter what his initial intent, he knew that if his fingers touched the soft skin of her neck, the anger would turn into a caress. That would certainly put the cat among the pigeons.

A knock sounded at the study door. Chas' heart leaped at the thought it might be Sam seeking him out to either apologize or maybe argue a little more. He would welcome either, he realized.

"Come."

But instead of Sam, his estate manager, John Weekes, let himself into the room. Chas' lips tightened a little at the smell of beer emanating from the man.

"John," Chas forced heartiness into his voice that he didn't feel, and gestured to the chair in front of his desk. Maybe his day hadn't been so good either.

"Evening," John said. "We didn't expect to see you here this week." He launched into a somewhat rambling explanation of why certain matters hadn't been seen to yet, and made a couple of suggestions for Chas' approval.

Chas nodded, and said what was appropriate. John had been a good estate manager once, and his instincts were still strong. Unfortunately, the carryings on of Chas' father, and to be honest, Chas' own neglect of his inheritance had probably caused the man to become disheartened. With a twinge of guilt, Chas realized it was one thing to delegate; quite another to leave one's employees to their own devices.

Of course with someone like Sam, oversight didn't seem to matter. Even now, he would trust her to do her job.

Which brought him back to the man before him. Chas sighed. Whatever plans he had for the estate, he was honour-bound to ensure that the house and the land were properly managed, and the employees, particularly the Weekes, were looked after.

Chas brought the conversation back to the beginning.

Once he'd determined that there was no body shop nearby capable of handling the repairs to an automobile like his, Chas said good night to John, and made a note to call London in the morning.

Alone again, Chas watched the play of light across his desk; the same desk used by his father, and his father before him. As a child, Chas had avoided this room; it held nothing for him but fear. A raging, demented grandfather who, in today's world, would likely have been in a nursing home. And a father whose mocking ways only made him appear less of a man, not more. Giving up, his society mother had absconded for a new life in America twenty-five years ago, leaving her eleven-year-old son to cope on his own. School holidays had been spent with Lionel, as his father now wished to be called by his only child, and his endless string of unsuitable women.

What a legacy.

Determined to never act with such cruel arrogance and irresponsibility, Chas had moved to London, rebuilt Burton-Porter, and learned to keep a tight rein on his emotions. But the only real way to distance himself from the pain of his family's past was to sell up, leaving Porter Hall and its history behind.

How naive to think that having Samantha Redfern at his side even if it was for only a few days would make his decision any easier.

So far, her presence seemed to have had the opposite effect. Her reaction to Burton Park, and then the hall, had given him a pride of place, something he had never experienced before.

That didn't excuse his behaviour. He should have been upfront with Sam, told her at the outset where they were headed and why. Too many years spent keeping his personal and professional lives separate had obviously taken their toll.

He reached for his whiskey and took a long slow sip.

He had a sudden flash of Sam stamping her feet at the auction hall. Full of fire when she was roused; cool and competent on the job.

He had never met a woman like her.

At lunch, when he told her he wanted to spend more time with her, he was speaking the truth. She did not have the elegant beauty and perfect demeanor of the women he had had relationships with in the past, but not one of them had ever affected him the way this stubborn, warm, talented woman had. It occurred to him that perhaps the reason she could spot the genuine article was because she *was* the genuine article.

Maybe that was why she had made that disastrous detour to the auction. It was incredibly rare to see a piece by such a fine silversmith. In the past, of course, if one had come on the open market, the family would swoop in and buy it back often using a third party. But this one had appeared so unexpectedly, he'd been caught off-guard. Funny that Sam should be the one bidding against him. Was it professional interest, he wondered, or something closer to home?

Chas frowned.

Sam knew as well as he did that provenance was an important part of their business. Knowing who owned a piece and when, could ratchet up the price tremendously. But the auction house had been unable to trace the candlestick's history.

Make that recent history, Chas reminded himself.

So where did Samantha Redfern fit in?

Stifling a yawn, Chas got to his feet. There was nothing more he could do tonight. Burton Park had stood unscathed for centuries; it was a glorious swath of land and wood and it would still be there when he woke up in the morning.

Pity it had to go.

His mother would rail against him selling his birthright. But that was no longer any of her concern. When he'd come of age, Chas had added to the divorce settlement Sylvia Porter, now Harker, had received from his father. He totally understood her decision to put as much distance as possible between herself and her first husband. Since then he had refused her continued financial requests.

But enough of that for now. In the morning, he would make amends for being less than forthright with Sam; he would show her around the estate, and maybe even take her for a ride.

And then they would have a chat.

About candlesticks.

And all things Samantha Redfern.

It was no use, thought Sam, she couldn't sleep. The cup of tea and two shortbread cookies Mrs. Weekes had brought up to her, had taken the edge off her hunger, but that was not enough to keep her going through the night. Plucking her cashmere shawl from the foot of the bed, Sam wrapped it around her shoulders. The thin nightgown she wore would be no match for the cool night air.

A soft breeze was ruffling the curtains. Sam padded over to the window and snugged the lock down on the casement.

The sun had long disappeared beneath the horizon but in its place, the moon cast its own particular brightness across the fields. So different from the hustle and bustle of the city, thought Sam. An owl hooted in the distance. For a girl who had grown up in a two-bedroom clapboard house, Porter Hall was the stuff of dreams.

Or was it nightmares?

As she turned, she caught sight of her own reflection in the dressing table mirror, soft and wide-eyed with the candlestick in the foreground. It looked at home on the dressing table, thought Sam, probably because when Porter Hall was first built, there would have been no electricity or gas.

She had originally set the candlestick atop the ornate fireplace on the far side of the room but that had made her feel sad. If her grandmother had remained in service instead of abruptly emigrating to Canada, it would have been someone like her who cleaned the hearth before the sun was up and tended the fire at night.

Sam frowned.

Romance for one meant hard work for someone else.

Like Mrs. Weekes.

Remembering the promise of a plate of sandwiches downstairs, Sam was suddenly quite ravenous.

She went to the door and gingerly turned its handle. Grateful, it didn't squeal, Sam looked up and down the dark hallway. The moon shining in the window at the end of the corridor cast long, distorted shadows. Telling herself not to be such a ninny, Sam stepped out into the corridor and closed the door behind her.

And felt the familiar tingle of childhood, sneaking about in the dark, tiptoeing past her grandmother's door barely able to suppress the giggles as she and her best friend went on a midnight raid. Knowing that her grandmother likely knew exactly what was going on, never lessened the adventure.

As she glided down the half-lit corridor, Sam felt such a frisson of excitement that when her stomach gurgled, she froze and then laughed at her own folly.

Thirty-one-years-old and as giddy as a schoolgirl.

She skipped down the main staircase. The flagstone floor was as cold as ice. She sprinted to the thick carpet a few steps away and followed its path.

Had Mrs. Weekes said the second door on the right?

Or the left.

Left. A strip of light showed ahead; the door was ajar. Sam pushed it open with the tips of her fingers and peered around the corner. Definitely the dining room.

And, on the sideboard, a platter full of sandwiches under a glass dome. And…Sam's nose twitched...there was coffee. And a carafe of tea, of course.

She started with a cup of coffee and then quickly scoffed two ham and cheese sandwiches. The bread was fresh and well-buttered, the ham thickly sliced and the cheddar was old and sharp and left a trail of crumbs.

She studied the plate while she ate. The display of sandwiches was uneven; someone had been here before her. Chas most likely. She topped up her coffee. He was probably brooding somewhere about the castle or maybe walking the parapets, whatever they were. Not that she had any interest in seeing him.

She set her cup down and reached for an egg and cress, nibbling carefully as she strolled about the room. Three enormous windows, or maybe they were French doors, dominated the far wall, draped from floor-to-ceiling in a pale yellow silk with repeating peacock designs. All fourteen dining chairs were covered in the same material and placed at precisely the same distance from the perfectly polished mahogany table. The centre of the table was dominated by a huge silver epergne showing a scene with elephants carrying rajas while servants waved fans. It had probably been acquired during the India trade. Smiling wryly, Sam wondered if it had been acquired as a symbol of the family's growing social status. During her years in the fine art business, Sam had seen many beautiful pieces and visited all the museums and estate houses she could, but never had she been in a private home like this.

She was slightly awed. Make that incredibly awed.

The carriage clock on the mantelpiece struck midnight as Sam swallowed the last of her coffee, belatedly wondering if it was decaf.

Regardless, it was time for bed.

But not before she had one last look around.

A rosewood cabinet with brass fittings drew her eye. It was not unlike a piece which had come up for auction in London last spring stood in the far corner of the dining room, its delicate lines almost lost in the shadows.

Furniture wasn't Sam's forte but she recognized the cabinet as either Regency or Georgian. Up close, it was even more exquisite.

The key was in the lock.

It was solid brass. As was the escutcheon plate behind it. Which, on closer inspection, proved to be badly scratched. If a servant had been responsible for such carelessness, they would have been dismissed on the spot.

Curious, Sam reached for the key. It felt warm in her hand. She turned it to the right and heard the snick of the lock a split second before she heard the voice behind her.

"Looking for something?" drawled Chas.

Sam's head fell forward and she dropped her hand.

A perfect end to a perfect day.

She drew in a breath and turned round to see Chas leaning against the door jam. "This is becoming a bad habit," she said.

"Of mine?" Chas quirked a black brow. "Or yours?" He took a few steps into the room and paused, his face almost expressionless, only his eyes gleaming in the half-light.

A rush of heat suffused Sam's face as she became suddenly conscious of the silky blue nightgown she wore beneath her shawl. That was *all* she wore beneath the shawl. Which immediately slipped off her right shoulder. Chas' eyes fell along with it coming to rest on her right breast.

Hidden by the thinnest of material.

Which was held up by the thinnest of straps. *Why* hadn't she packed her pyjama pants and a t-shirt? Maybe because she'd expected to be alone in the climate controlled room of a five-star hotel in New York, not confronting the mysterious lord of the manor in an ancient country house – at midnight. Sam fought a sudden hysterical urge to giggle. Instead, she tugged her wrap back where it belonged and held it tightly against her chest.

"I see you've finished your business," she charged.

Chas cleared his throat. "For the moment." The corner of his mouth twitched as he raised his gaze to meet her scowl. He advanced further into the room. "Do you know that before today I'd never seen you in anything other than a charcoal suit or a demure little black dress with pearls. And now this…not conventional of course, but I must say I approve."

The light from the sideboard threw his shadow across the room so that it lay at her feet. Her bare feet. Sam curled her toes in embarrassment. "Actually, I was about to leave."

"Finished poking about have we?" His eyes were almost black in the half-light.

Sam fought the flush of guilt but it was, as always, written all over her face. The set of his jaw showed her that he had seen, and correctly interpreted her reaction.

"I beg your pardon?" Sam asked, feigning innocence. "I just put the key back in. It had dropped out."

You'll never be a good liar, her grandmother had told her, clucking her tongue when Sam tried to get away with an extra cookie or when she was older, an illicit cigarette. Her complexion was a telltale she had inherited from her mother, a slight flush that would start at the base of her neck and rise to the roots of her hair.

Chas Porter was a completely different judge.

"This cabinet," she cleared her throat, "it's rosewood, isn't it? Like the Regency cabinet we have coming up for auction next month."

"You've broadened your area of expertise." Chas moved closer.

Sam picked up a hint of whiskey. Chas still wore the oxford cloth shirt he'd had on earlier. There was not an after shave, nor cologne nor musk in a bottle that could compete with the intoxicating scent of warm cotton, male testosterone and well-aged whiskey.

Her own breath, on the other hand, was ragged.

Sam shrank back. In London where the Chas Porter she knew neatly fit into everyone's perception of an unemotional, cold, calculating yet devilishly handsome boss, it had been far easier not to see the intense reality of this man.

The brass key nudged into the small of her back.

"I…I haven't actually agreed to work with you yet," she stammered.

Chas head cocked to one side. "I don't remember you having any choice. Slight thing with that candlestick we were both after. We really must talk about that. The silversmith's wife was equally talented as I recall."

He moved in still closer, and his scent became stronger. Her heart was speeding up. The air between them had thickened with the silence between their words. The sound of their breathing.

Sam nodded, her mouth suddenly dry. "Hattie," she whispered. "Her name was Hattie. She specialized in small work, teaspoons, buckles."

Chas ran his hands gently over the gleaming wood of the cabinet. "You do know your history, don't you?" His lips barely brushed the top of her hair. "Only the inlays are satinwood by the way," he murmured tracing the fine grain of the wood with his fingertip, "the carcass is rosewood. Superb craftsmanship, don't you think?"

He was so close, Sam could feel the heat coursing through her veins.

She had goals and dreams and an agenda he mustn't know about; getting involved with Chas Porter was not an option. Not now. And not ever.

Despite the temptation.

And the nearness of his mouth as he bent his head towards her.

With a fierce will, she ducked under his arm.

A mixture of disappointment and relief rolled over her when he didn't press his suit. Yet neither of them made a move for the door.

Chas swung around to face her.

She stepped back, clasped her shawl with her left hand and steadied herself with her right, resting it on the curved back of a nearby chair. "You must be really tired," she said desperately, "after everything that happened today…"

"Do you mean the strain of your embezzlement or the destruction done to my car?" The chill had crept back into his voice, but Sam was determined to broach the subject. If she didn't, it would be hanging out there for them, not that she expected to be with Burton-Porter much longer.

"Actually," Sam said, "I wanted to say I was sorry if my behaviour didn't seem entirely professional."

Her apology was met with several long moments of silence.

Sam gnawed her lower lip.

The next few words out of his mouth might very well determine her future.

"You do realize you'll have to make good those losses," said Chas. He moved into the light and she could see that his eyes weren't cold at all. In fact, he almost looked feverish. "On the other hand, you could just marry me."

"Marry you!"

Sam's jaw dropped.

And so did her shawl.

"You have got to be kidding."

Chas smiled. "I thought I was," he said raking her with his eyes, "but not anymore."

Sam instinctively raised her hand.

Chas grabbed her wrist, the firm warmth of his fingers gently holding her in his grasp. She should have pulled away. She could have, easily. But instead she stood there, gazing up at the face of the man who had fought with her, laughed at her and tormented her. Made her feel more alive than anyone she had ever met. His scent filled her nostrils. The gleam of his eyes dove into her very being. She should have run away. But instead she stepped closer.

His hands slid up her bare arms to the milky whiteness of her shoulders. She leaned into him, her palms pressed against his chest, feeling the rough fabric of his shirt and the hard muscles beneath. Then her arms reached up and wrapped themselves around his neck, just as his hands dropped down around her waist to pull her hard against him. Unconsciously, she lifted her face. For a moment her eyes slid over the strong line of his jaw, the high cheekbones and firm lips that made Chas Porter the handsomest man she had ever seen. Then he leaned down to meet her desire, at first gently, brushing her mouth tenderly with his lips and then as the heat rose and crackled between them, pressing his mouth demandingly against hers.

She moaned softly, opening her lips to invite him closer and he responded. His kiss became harder, more insistent. All of Sam's senses swirled into that one perfect kiss. Clinging to him, wanting more and more, a small voice hidden deeply within her began to protest. Sam clung to Chas and then with a groan, wrenched herself away.

She grabbed up her discarded shawl and again wrapped it tightly around her.

Chas leaned against the cabinet and scrubbed a hand fiercely over his face. He forced a smile.

"Shall I take that as a yes or as a no?"

Using all her willpower, Sam straightened her shoulders. "Good night, Mr. Porter."

"Miss Redfern."

One last lingering look, and then she tore from the dining room.

She sped through the entrance hall over the icy flagstones, up the stairs and down the darkened corridor. It wasn't until the door to the guest room was well and truly closed behind her that she realized she hadn't actually said no.

Damn and blast the man.
No way she was going to marry him!
Not even if he was the last man on earth.
Then why, Samantha dear, is your mouth dry, your heart pounding and your loins throbbing with desire?

Telling herself, a.k.a. the goddess of single women, to shut it, Samantha Redfern dove under the covers and turned out the light. But it was a long time before she fell asleep.

Five

Chas was waiting for her in the stable yard, Mrs. Weekes had told her, as she presented Sam with a breakfast tray of tea, croissant, and a poached egg. A pair of riding boots dangled precariously under the housekeeper's left arm.

"And he hates to be kept waiting. But I guess you know that already," she added with a wry smile. "He set off to fetch the horses about an hour ago."

Sam smiled an acknowledgement, but said nothing as Mrs. Weekes set the boots down at the foot of the bed and produced a pair of riding gloves to go with them before she bustled away. It had taken Sam ages to fall asleep last night and she was loath to get into a conversation with the housekeeper. The searing kiss she had shared with Chas had left her in a fever of longing and indecision. She was an interloper in a grand house, and the housekeeper's presence had reinforced that one irrefutable fact. Chas Porter might be the most exciting man she had ever met, but he was her boss. And she should never, ever forget that he was the one who had tricked her into coming to his home in the country.

Her eyes flickered across the room to the candlestick.

Not that she was without guilt. Another fact she would do well to remember.

Suddenly anxious to be outside, Sam drained the last of her tea and threw back the duvet.

Her wardrobe had not been planned for a week in the country, so the best she could do was jeans and a beaded sweater. It might be a bit too chic for a gallop. Sam shrugged. But it would have to do. She picked up the boots and examined them.

Beautifully made, hardly used, and designed for a more delicate foot than Sam possessed. Grimacing, she forced her feet into the boots and stuck the gloves in her pocket.

Finding her way through the house, Sam blinked as she stepped through the terrace doors and into the gentle sunshine of mid-morning. Rolling lawns spread before her. Beds of old roses in desperate need of a good pruning defined the formal flagstone terrace. Their current neglect was a sad reflection of just how unhappy a house Porter Hall had become. She was beginning to suspect a well-hidden pain behind Chas' cool exterior. But that, she reminded herself sharply, was none of her business.

Chas was on the far side of the stable yard, standing, with his back to her. He looked magnificent in his boots and riding clothes, like a modern-day Mr. Darcy. Remembering the night before, Sam's breath quickened. How was she going to face him? Ducking behind the garden wall, Sam watched Chas cinch the saddle of a massive chestnut while another, smaller horse waited nearby, his reddish-brown coat glistening in the sun. If this moment was her penalty for outbidding the boss, Sam thought, then she was deliriously happy.

And no longer tired despite her restless night full of erotic dreams and unfulfilled desires that, until yesterday, were unimaginable. Before last night, Sam had always believed that those kinds of daydreams were for the beautiful. That she would be better off hoping for a man who would appreciate her for who she was and come to know her passionate side. She never would have guessed that a single kiss could rouse her to such unsuspected heights.

The memory brought a soft smile to her lips as she admired the snug fit of Chas' breeches, the fine leather of his riding boots, and the broad reach of his muscular back and shoulders. She couldn't wait to see him in the saddle.

Chiding herself for being a silly goose, Sam left the security of the wall and strode across the cobblestone courtyard with forced confidence. She might look like a waif in yesterday's jeans and today's borrowed boots, but she'd never felt as womanly as she did that morning.

Until Chas dropped the saddle flap and turned towards her.

The scowl on his face was so fierce, she came to a crashing halt.

"I see Mrs. Weekes gave you my message." He said it in a tone so matter-of-fact Sam knew in an instant she'd made a terrible mistake – nothing between them had changed. She'd forgotten her place and now he was determined to return her to where she rightfully belonged. Not an equal – an employee, with neither fame nor fortune. This was so not what she was expecting after last night's intimacy. The depth of Chas' kiss had gone way beyond light flirtation with nothing between them but a slip of a nightgown.

Sam hesitated, then straightened her spine. Well, phooey, on him. He wasn't the only one who could play this game. Times had changed even if this lord of the manor had not.

She might want to kick herself for being such a romantic fool, but she would be damned if she'd let Chas Porter see how hurt she was.

"And good morning, to you, too," she snapped, neatly sidestepping him. From the back pocket of her jeans, she pulled the gloves Mrs. Weekes had given her and tugged them on as she walked towards the stables.

The smaller horse shone with good health. Saddled and waiting, she saw his ears prick forward at her approach and slowed. He seemed placid enough, but Sam knew she needed to take a calming breath.

"And what's your name?" she cooed. He swung his magnificent head towards her showing the flash of white between his huge brown eyes.

Sam heard footsteps.

"Max," said Chas. "His name is Max."

"Hello, Max," said Sam softly. She reached up and gently stroked his gleaming coat. Max rewarded her with such a soft whinny, she could have wept. As if sensing her distress, he lowered his nose and nuzzled her neck.

Sam breathed in the familiar aroma of horse and hay. It had been years since she'd ridden a horse, but the pungent smell took her back to her childhood, following her grandfather around as he trained high-bred horses at Woodbine race track. Little girls rarely got to even sit on the back of one of those magnificent creatures, but she had always felt comfortable around them, and instinctively knew Max was the one for her. He nodded his agreement as she stroked his long neck.

"You seem to have made a conquest," said Chas, drawing up behind her, his scent mingling with horse and leather. It was overwhelmingly male. And beyond reach.

Sam tamped down the lump in her throat, and turned to face her boss.

"Thank you," she said simply. "He's a beautiful horse."

Their gazes met this time and held, a thousand signals flying between them without a single word spoken. Chas cleared his throat. "I thought if we went for a ride, we could put a bit of distance between yesterday's…adventures and getting down to work."

What he really means, Sam thought miserably, is us. The flirtatious banter, the sparring with the boss, it all had to go. She was saddened by his words, but somehow consoled by the thought that he was acknowledging the emotional spark they had shared the night before. It went beyond the physical attraction and into dangerous territory. Territory she had always carefully avoided in her past. She did not intend to ever be at the mercy of anyone. This was the 21st century! Chas might be her boss, but he was not her master and commander.

"Good plan," she replied keeping her voice as neutral as possible.

It might pain her to bury her feelings for him, but better to do it now before they could blossom beyond her control. She had already jeopardized her career; she was not going to risk her heart. A truce, no matter how uneasy, was in order. For both their sakes.

Chas reached past her for Max's bridle. "That big bruiser over there is Damien, by the way," he said leading Max into the open expanse of the stable yard. "Can you manage while I fetch a couple of helmets?" He handed the reins to her. She nodded and he headed to the tack room.

"So what do you think, Max?" Sam murmured.

But the chestnut had nothing to say. They stood together companionably until Chas returned a few moments later wearing a helmet and holding one out for her.

"Try this one for size," he said.

Sam surrendered the reins and took the hard hat from Chas. It was surprisingly lightweight. She tucked her hair up and after a few minor adjustments, snapped the chin strap and snugged it into place.

Chas placed his hands on either side of her helmet and gave it a wiggle. "How does that feel?"

Sam swallowed. "Perfect."

"You missed a piece," he said reaching for a strand of her hair. He slipped it under her helmet, then stepped back to assess his handiwork. "Nervous?"

All Sam could do was shake her head. "I'm fine."

He nodded, satisfied. Chas might be over their shared passion, but the memory of that kiss still thrummed in her blood. How on earth she was going to retain her composure around him, when those broad shoulders and his intoxicating scent demanded that she fold into his arms and feel the protective strength of his muscles? She had no idea now how to deal with him. It had been so much easier when he was simply her boss. Just that brief brush of his fingers, was enough to rebuild the fire banked in her belly. A moment of pure silence engulfed them, broken a moment later by Max's snort and tossed head. He was ready to gallop through this glorious morning, even if these two puzzling humans were not.

"Okay, Max, we hear you," said Chas. He looked down at Sam.

"Ready?" he asked.

"Ready," she croaked. Last night was nothing but a brief encounter with a feudal lord. A modern man, the head of Burton-Porter, faced her this morning.

"Good. Let's get you in the saddle. I'll need to adjust the stirrups."

"I can do it," she told him. "I'm fine."

"No." Chas drew the reins over Max's head. "We do it my way," he declared in a tone that brooked no argument.

Sam had no choice. She all but snatched the reins from Chas, gripping them tightly with her left hand as she reached for the saddle.

"Left leg," ordered Chas moving in behind her. Sam felt his strong shoulder press into the middle of her back as he bent down and cupped his hands.

It took all her concentration not to picture him behind her as she lowered herself into his care. But the image was overwhelming and fraught with overtones. Heaven forbid Max should sense the rush of her heartbeat as she felt Chas' hands support her. It was almost comical.

"Easy, boy," murmured Chas as Sam concentrated her weight onto her right leg. If she'd been a drama queen, she could feign distress and slide down into his arms, weeping with fear. Sadly, that was not her style. Besides, she was excited at the prospect of riding again, no matter what the circumstances.

"Up you go."

On Chas' command, she sprang up and into the saddle.

Max shifted uneasily. Damn, thought Sam. She was shaking. She willed herself to sit calmly while Chas positioned her foot in the stirrup.

"How are the boots?" he asked.

"A little tight." Her toes were pinched together. But then the boots had probably belonged to one of Chas' old girlfriends, who would have been, Sam thought bitterly, slim, willowy, and a perfect rider. With lots of money, judging by the buttery softness of the gloves. Or perhaps more than one of Chas' women had worn them. "Left behind, were they?"

Chas tugged on the strap and glanced up at her. His eyes narrowed. "If you must know, those boots you are wearing belonged to a woman named Daphne. She was blonde and spectacularly beautiful. Unfortunately, she had the brain of a gnat and even lower morals than my father… how's that feel?" he asked.

"Fine." squeaked Sam.

"…so low, she thought it might be fun," Chas added as he went around to adjust the other stirrup, "to tease a naïve seventeen-year-old. That would be me."

Sam didn't know what to say. She opened her mouth, then closed it again, and sat there feeling like the fool that she was while Chas fiddled with the leathers. Her flash of anger had died down, giving way to empathy for that eager, humiliated boy.

"Try that." Sam dutifully slid her boot into the stirrup. He buckled the straps into place and then mounted up.

Sam snuck a peek at Chas' near-perfect physique. No surprise, he mounted Damien with ease. The stallion pranced and reared playfully. Chas' muscles rippled beneath his tight-fitting clothes as he controlled the magnificent creature with ease. The sight of the sun gleaming on the velvety coat of the horse and the interplay of two magnificent specimens made the breath catch in Sam's throat.

"That's enough now," Chas murmured.

The big horse snorted in response and Max's head shot up.

Sam loosened the reins. Max crossed the yard and fell into step with Damien, their hooves clopping contentedly as Chas took the lead from the stable yard across a swath of grass.

"How do you keep them exercised when you're in London?" Sam asked. She knew animals like this needed more than a comfortable box stall and paddock.

"They're stabled at a horse farm a few miles from here," he explained, "but when I'm home, they're with me. Which, unfortunately, is not often enough…" he added. "Horses were by far the best part of my boyhood."

Remembering her own losses, buffered by the sure protection of her grandparents Sam gazed at Chas with new understanding. He could have gone the route of his father and grandfather, but instead he had thrown himself into rebuilding the business, rebuilding the name he had inherited.

Chas swung towards Sam. "How are you feeling?"

"Apologetic."

"You weren't to know," said Chas. "At least it will help you understand why I might want to catalogue the estate." He shifted in the saddle. "In fact, your little escapade yesterday solved a major problem for me. I now have an expert who is not connected to the Hall, and whose judgment I trust."

"Really?" Sam glanced over at him.

"Really." Chas smiled wryly. "I might keep my distance at Burton-Porter, but it doesn't mean I don't know you are both discreet and professional."

They walked on in silence. The gentle sway of the horse beneath her became more and more soothing. Chas Porter was a complex man with a complicated history, Sam realized. There must not be any more intimacies for both their sakes. But perhaps they could become friends.

"How are you feeling now?" asked Chas.

When she saw how blue his eyes were, the answer was easy. "Great." And, suddenly she was.

She was on a horse somewhere in Derbyshire with a man who she knew would look after her. Bruise her heart in the process, maybe, but he would ensure she came to no harm while she was in his care.

Chas kept the pace at a slow walk until they were well beyond the stables.

Burton Park unfolded in front of them, its formal lawns giving way to a soft green meadow which sloped away from the manor house. Sam gave herself permission to enjoy the day and raised her face to the wind.

"Shall we pick up the pace a bit?"

Sam smiled. "Yes, please."

As they crossed the meadow at a slow canter, Sam knew she'd made the right decision to follow the threads of her childhood back to England.

No matter where she ended up.

If only life were always this simple, thought Chas, as he watched Sam's beautifully rounded bottom rise and fall in the saddle ahead of him. He had purposely dropped back to give her a bit of space, but the sight of her perfect curves held him in thrall. Ever since she had melted so wonderfully into his arms the night before, he'd been unable to focus on anything else. This ride was supposed fix that, to clear their heads, and create a companionable distance. But when Sam chuckled at the antics of a scolding squirrel and turned her head to catch Chas' reaction, he realized he was already in deep, deep trouble. How had he not been aware until yesterday, how full of life this woman was; he'd hired her for heaven's sake! And then kept his distance. Why?

Wrenching his thoughts back to safer ground, Chas cast a critical eye over Sam's ability in the saddle. He needn't have bothered. She rode well. Max was the perfect mount, and Sam was proving to be a natural, instinctively understanding the balance between controlling the horse and giving him his head. Maybe he should take lessons from Max, thought Chas ruefully. Despite his best intentions, his ill humour had jeopardized his relationship with Sam. All he'd wanted to do was put it back on a professional keel, but he had so little experience with women who touched him on a startlingly deep level, that he'd handled it all wrong.

Handled her all wrong.

Sam was saucy, stubborn and sexy. His eyes strayed to the boots she wore and grinned. And a tad jealous, maybe? She had definitely shown a spurt of temper over those boots. She would have known they weren't his mother's. Unfortunately, everyone at Burton-Porter knew the story. How his mother had cleared Porter Hall of everything she owned and then some, a week before she left for greener pastures. And that he rarely attended charity and business affairs without a beautiful woman on his arm. Obviously, Sam had drawn her own conclusion.

Chas purposely chose his dates wisely, and whether they liked it or not, the women in his world understood that his only commitment was to his business. Yet, in less than twenty-four hours, determined, passionate Sam had trampled over his boundaries. She had drawn things out of him that he had never, ever shared with anyone else. His housekeeper wasn't blind, and had often kept a close eye when Chas was home from boarding school, but she had never pried.

What then was it about Miss Redfern?

And his sudden need to be near her. Chas cleared the cobwebs from his head and urged Damien forward.

"It's so lovely," breathed Sam as he approached her side. "I don't see how you can bear to leave this for the hustle and bustle of London."

They had come to the rise above what was once the home farm and stopped to admire the view. He could see George on the near side of the next field mending a fence. His sheep dotted the slope beyond, their woolly bodies kept in check as usual by Robbie, George's sharp-eyed border collie.

"If you don't mind, I'd like to go down and say hello to George," he said.

"Is he the man we saw last night?" Sam flashed him a spectacular grin. "The one with the handkerchief."

Chas nodded. "That's the one." His expression darkened. "I want to have a word with him about my plans for the Hall…before he hears it from somebody else."

"Will he lose his land?"

Chas shook his head. "The home farm was deeded to him years ago. According to local legend, George's ancestors arrived here long before ours did."

"Ah, then he'll know every skeleton in the Burton-Porter closets." Sam grinned mischievously.

Chas groaned. "You have no idea. You wouldn't be thinking of adding blackmail to your rap sheet, would you, Ms. Redfern?"

Sam laughed and kicked Max to a canter. Chas rode beside her. Sharing his history with someone like Sam felt incredibly natural, as though they'd known each other for years. It was a thought that both comforted and unsettled him.

Hearing their approach above the sheep bleating in the field beyond, the old man straightened, rubbing his lower back as he turned to greet them. "Morning, George," said Chas.

"Morning." George tipped his cap, his gaze settling on Sam.

"Hello," said Sam.

George stepped forward as Chas made the introductions. "Pleased to meet you, Miss Redfern."

"Call me Sam," said Sam as she stretched out her gloved hand for George's calloused one. "I work for Mr. Porter. In London," she quickly added.

"That so?" George released Sam's hand and glanced at Chas. "Old paintings and the like, is it?"

Chas was opening his mouth to answer when he heard Sam laugh. "I can tell a Gainsborough from a Turner," she proceeded to tell George, "but my speciality is antique silver."

"Then you've come to the right place," said the old man his gaze lingering on Chas for a moment before shifting back to Sam.

Before the conversation could go any further, Chas took charge. "There's something I need to talk to you about, George…"

"Aye, laddie. I believe there is…" he replied without turning.

Damn, thought Chas, no wonder George was out of sorts when they spoke last evening. Evelyn Weekes, or more likely her husband, John, had alerted the man that there were changes ahead. Having Sam by his side confirmed it.

But sly old George was busy chatting to Sam. "You're sure you've never ridden Max before?"

Sam smiled down at him and patted the horse's gleaming neck. "I haven't been on horseback for years."

"Then you must have a bit of the Irish in you," the old smoothie added, "Chas' grandfather wouldn't have a groom from anywhere but Ireland. Isn't that right, Chas?" he said over his shoulder.

"My grandfather was from Ireland…originally," Sam cut in, unconsciously tucking a tendril of auburn hair back under her helmet while she spoke. "And when I was a little girl, he worked at a racetrack in Toronto."

"Is that so," mused George.

His keen and well-weathered eyes met Sam's, but then he turned to Chas with a question of a muddy field that needed to be drained.

Relieved, Chas dismounted, tied Damien's reins loosely to the fence and the two walked off for a few moments to discuss the farm's needs. Sam sat still, gazing outward at the brilliant green land, and absently stroking Max's velvet neck. She passed over George's hint, to the memory of the Irish lilt in her grandfather's voice. He'd met her grandmother in England, that she knew, and somehow the candlestick they had brought with them to Canada had come into play.

Wouldn't that be ironic, thought Sam, if they had worked in the area at one time. She looked towards Chas tramping the field alongside the old farmer; seeing Chas hold his pace to accommodate George's slower gait warmed her heart. His athletic grace and his courtesy marked him as a true gentleman. Just watching him made the breath catch in Sam's throat. Face it, Sam, she chided herself, it doesn't matter how wild your dreams get, this is your boss you're drooling over. She had seen the women he'd brought to company functions and the charity auctions they held. Only rarely had he escorted the same woman twice. If none of them had been able to hold his attention for more than a week or two, what chance did she have? You're a full blown idiot, she told herself. You know very well a hint of passion does not a relationship make and no amount of wishful thinking will make it any different.

When Chas returned, his mouth was drawn into a tight line and George was scowling. Apparently the news that the house might be sold had not gone down well. As Chas swung himself into the saddle, George stroked Max's nose. He smiled wryly up at Sam.

"He's a good lad," he told her quietly. She thought he was going to say more, but he held back.

"Maybe we'll see each other again sometime," Sam said impulsively.

"I hope so," said George. He tipped his cap in farewell. Sam waited as he ambled back to his fence.

Max was chomping at the bit so she nudged him gently and they turned to follow Chas and Damien.

A short while later, they were skirting the back of the estate with Chas in the lead, heading towards the woods Sam had seen from her window the night before. When they reached a path by a tree-shaded stream, Sam held back, sensing that Chas' need to be alone. For better or worse, Porter Hall was his home. It had been in his family for generations and now he was thinking about letting it go. His feelings must run deeper than he'd let on; she wondered briefly about his teenage encounter with his father's mistress, but decided it had to be far more complicated than that. For a man so committed to restoring the family business and protecting the Burton-Porter name, it seemed odd to her that he would choose to abandon his family heritage.

Ahead of her, Damien's trot had been kicked into a canter and then a gallop as Chas relieved his anger in time-honoured fashion. Maybe she was reading him the wrong way, thought Sam. Maybe what he needed was a friend. He'd spent half his life alone, and he was about to make a decision that would change that life forever!

Forgetting how long it had been since she'd done any serious riding, Sam urged Max to a faster pace. She and Chas weren't exactly friends, but that didn't mean she couldn't be supportive. She should be by his side. Besides, she might never get a chance to ride a horse like this again. Leaning over the neck of the magnificent animal, she flew along the path untethered, revelling in a sense of freedom as she raced through the crisp green countryside.

The gap closed.

The path curved and she lost sight of Chas.

They were so close to the stream, she could see her reflection as she and Max tore through the underbrush, hooves thundering and spirits soaring as Chas and Damien came back into view. And then suddenly, it all went bad. A panicked rabbit darted across their path. Max reared, and

Sam found herself truly flying through the air. A sickeningly brief sight of spinning green ended in a jarring thud as she crashed into the bank of the stream.

Max's sharp whinny brought Chas up short. He jerked Damien around and tore back down the path to where Sam lay unmoving on the ground. He flung himself from the saddle and kneeled beside her.

"Sam," he called. "Sam, can you hear me?"

She opened one mud-encrusted eye and then closed it again. "I think George was wrong about the Irish," she groaned.

"Where does it hurt? Can you get up?" Chas gripped her hand, afraid to move her in case there were serious injuries.

"It hurts in too many places to name," Sam murmured. "And my pride. My pride is damaged beyond redemption." Her right eye fluttered open. "I think the mud saved the rest of me. Thoughtful of you to put the mud right here." She sighed. "Isn't this where the handsome prince kisses the princess and makes it all better."

"Absolutely," said Chas.

But it was Max who leaned over her and snorted, his whiskers brushing her face with slobber.

"Yeow!" Sam shot into a sitting position. "Okay. Serves me right. Now my pride is completely shattered."

Chas exploded with laughter.

"You, Miss Redfern, are full of surprises…but, seriously, are you sure you're all right?"

"I'm fine, Chas. A little stunned, but nothing's broken." She wiggled her fingers for emphasis and then smiled at him, the sun twinkling in her eyes and the laughter bringing a glow to her cheeks that no cosmetic could ever achieve.

Still, Chas assessed her carefully. He should never have left her. He saw the splash of mud on her forehead, the way her hair twisted wildly from underneath her helmet and that tiny sprinkle of freckles across her nose. Without doubt, he concluded, she was the most beautiful woman he had ever seen.

"I'm not a prince," he murmured, "but I do want to make it all better."

Eyes locking on hers, he leaned in for a soft kiss. He did not demand as he had the night before; he offered the sweetness of his lips, fuelled by the admiration that was growing in him for this unexpected woman. He felt her hesitate only a second and then she drew herself toward him, her hand slowly reaching for his shoulder. His kiss became firmer, more demanding and joyfully she parted her lips to take in as much of him as he offered. The earthiness of their surroundings mingled with Sam's natural freshness. She wound her arms around his neck. Chas pulled her closer to him relishing the soft curves of her body, the supple firmness of her form. His kiss became stronger and deeper; his hands stroked her back, their passions twined. Dimly, he knew he should pull back, stop himself. But he had never been as drawn to any woman as to Sam…his employee…off limits…

The thought froze as twelve-hundred pounds of horseflesh bumped his shoulder hard, propelling him forward. With a woof, Sam landed back into the mud, only this time Chas was on top of her.

"Apparently," he drawled, "our behaviour is unbecoming."

He glanced back to see his massive chestnut had joined his buddy by the stream. Their big brown eyes looked on disapprovingly as Chas reluctantly rolled off Sam and drew her to her feet. She reached up to wipe a streak of mud from his face. He caught her by the wrist. "Are you really all right?" he asked.

"Perfect," she said. Her eyes slid beyond him. "But we do have the most unusual chaperones."

Their eyes met again, and Chas felt his pulse speed up, but Sam shook her head.

"I don't know how we're going to explain this to Mrs. Weekes," she said brushing ineffectually at the mud caking her backside.

Fighting a feeling of rejection, Chas pulled his eyes away and reached for Damien's reins. "Unfortunately, I think Mrs. Weekes will figure things out without any kind of explanation."

Sam's smile suddenly became brittle. "Seen this before, has she?" She grabbed Max's reins and leading him to a fallen tree, stood on it while she gingerly raised herself into the saddle.

Chas mounted up and walked Damien beside the seething Sam. "No, never from me," he said evenly. "It's obvious there is an attraction between us." He hesitated. "But I do have to apologize… again. There's been no excuse for my behavior. You are my employee and should not be subjected to this." His words were harsh, but they had to be said.

He urged Damien ahead of Sam, not wanting her to see his embarrassment, and above all, not wanting her to see how much he yearned to take her in his arms. But he was not his father or his grandfather. He owed it to her to protect her – even from himself.

They rode this way to the stable yard, Sam slightly behind him and stonily silent. Wearily, Chas wished that he had not made such a muddle of things, had not let his attraction for her drive his actions. Every example in his life shouted that letting passion rule led to emotional and financial disaster. He had almost repaired the financial disaster. He didn't know how to repair the emotional mayhem. The honourable thing would be to discharge Sam's debt, and let her go, candlestick and all. He was quite capable of dealing with his own estate. But he couldn't bear the thought of staying at the Hall without her. He needed her help, but most of all, he needed her. He swung off Damien and silently steadied Sam as she slid down from Max. "Go on in and clean up," he told her. "I'll groom the horses."

She smiled but her eyes were like ice chips. "Good idea," she said. "I'll take the back stairs. Throw Mrs. Weekes off the scent. And maybe, when I've showered and changed, we can meet in the library. I'll be Miss Redfern, and you can be Mr. Porter. And we can pretend that neither today, nor yesterday ever happened."

"Sam!" Chas called, but she had swept away toward the house trying desperately not to limp in her borrowed boots.

Six

The early evening sun was washing the cobblestones with streaks of pink and gold as Chas crossed the yard and entered the stables. He paused, letting the familiar cocoon of its shadowy interior wrap around him. There was no need to turn on any lights. Sam was exactly where he knew she'd be; in Max's stall making amends. He could hear the rustle of straw and the soft swish of the brush as she moved about currying Max's coat.

Shortly after they'd returned from their disastrous ride, Chas had sent a note of apology up to Sam's room, along with a pot of tea and fresh fruit, courtesy of Evelyn Weekes. She'd offered, and he'd thankfully agreed. Everything he had learned about "doing the right thing" had come from his housekeeper, not the self-centred actions of his parents. No matter how much fire sparked between him and Sam, Chas was determined to not be like his father nor his father before him. If he could keep Sam at a distance, it would be better for both of them. Her stubborn refusal to do as she was bid would certainly help that along, Chas thought wryly.

But regardless of any personal animosity that might exist between them, he'd been sufficiently worried about the tumble Sam had taken that morning to put off any thought of the work ahead of them. A hot bath and a restful afternoon might soothe both muscles and feelings. He knew his own were thoroughly bruised.

Standing stock still, he savoured the orderly peacefulness of the stable. It had always been a place of solace for him; he hoped it was for Sam as well. Oblivious to his presence, she crooned a soft tune as she fussed over Max. Chas was loath to interrupt, yet if he didn't announce his presence soon, they might get off on the wrong foot again and that was the last thing he wanted.

"Hello?" he called advancing down the line of stalls.

The singing stopped.

"Sam?" Chas repeated. "Are you in here?" Aside from Damien shifting his massive weight through the straw on the other side of the stable from Max, there was an absence of sound. Beyond the pounding of his heart, of course, which seemed to be playing havoc with his mind. He'd give her another few minutes to compose herself, he decided, then he would pull rank. He'd fought long and hard to become his own man, and no employee of his, no matter how enticing, was going to worm her way into his life, leaving him cautious and unsure of his next move.

Luckily, Sam chose that moment to step out of Max's stall. She was wearing an old sweater belonging to Mrs. Weekes, and held a brush in her hand. "Hi."

"Hi."

Now that she was in front of him, his hard stance slipped away. They stood a few paces apart assessing each other's moods. The silence seemed to stretch forever, then green eyes met his, and relaxed. Chas was rewarded with a tentative smile. "Thank you for letting me take the afternoon off," said Sam. "This morning's adventure was a bit of a shock." She cocked her head. "Pleasant, but shocking." she added.

Chas surged forward, saw the mischief written all over her face, and felt relief ripple through him. She was okay, she wasn't angry, and the world could go forward again.

"You did a great job on Max's coat," she continued. "I couldn't find a speck of mud anywhere."

"I spent most of my afternoon out here," Chas admitted, "currying the life out of both of them. It seems to have settled us all down," he added. He threw a puzzled glance towards Damien's stall. "Usually, at this time of night, I come in here and find two long faces…it's pathetic really the way they beg for attention. And treats." He grinned at her. "I'll bet Damien tossed his head towards that sack hanging outside the tack room until you took the hint."

"Ahh," said Sam. "He was determined, but it was Max batting his eyelashes that did me in. And how many apples did you give them this afternoon, Mr. Porter?" she teased.

"One or two…dozen," Chas admitted.

"They're pigs, not horses," laughed Sam. "Aren't you, Damien?" She asked as his big head swung over the rails at her approach.

Chas went to stand beside her. With her auburn hair up in a ponytail, and her ragamuffin outfit, it was hard to believe she wasn't still in her teens. A shaft of sunlight caught the sheen in her hair, he saw Sam for the natural beauty; she didn't need cosmetics and designer clothes. It wouldn't matter if she were mucking out the stable or shepherding a wealthy client around the silver department, she would be gracious and poised and…totally, totally desirable.

He rubbed Damien's whiskered muzzle. "Nice try," he told the big horse, "but your breath smells like cider."

"We did give them a good workout," he teased her.

"That we did." Suddenly, Sam's face puckered. She turned away and half-raised her arm to indicate she was going back to finish grooming Max who was making his displeasure known against the wooden sides of the stall.

"Sam…wait." Chas touched her lightly on the arm.

She twisted her face towards his, uncertainty written where a few minutes earlier, he'd seen pleasure, and he knew he was responsible for this myriad of feelings which had engulfed them since the second he'd picked her out at the auction hall. It was up to him to reassure her, to close the distance between them, and he had to do it now.

Before the damage was too deep.

"It's obvious we can't go back to the way things were before yesterday." Chas cleared his throat. Talking about how he felt was so much harder than having a conversation in his head. Here, in front of the woman who had unleashed a passionate longing he had never known before, he was as tongue-tied as a schoolboy. And about as emotionally mature. But those days were over. His urge to protect her overrode his natural reluctance to share his heart with anyone. He would say his piece. As a man who was finally, thanks to this woman, able to express his feelings, no matter how halting and awkward the delivery.

"...And I don't want to," he said finally, "but I do want us to be friends. Perhaps, under different circumstances, we could be more...I don't know what else to say...you're a beautiful woman and... hell, I don't know what else to say!"

He held his hand out. "Miss Samantha Redfern, would you please do me the honour of being my friend?" It sounded foolish to his ears and certainly wasn't the phrase he'd practised earlier, but it made Sam laugh.

And then her chin went up, and she stuck out her hand. "Yes, Mr. Porter," she said. "I would very much like to be your friend."

Her voice wavered, and he could have sworn her eyes were wet with tears as he took her hand in his, but he stood strong. He had to…they were close enough for him to sweep her into his arms and forget all her stubborn, cantankerous traits while he savoured the lushness of her lips once more.

He released her hand.

Dusk was throwing shadows into the corners of the stable. A dangerous desire to make love to this woman on a bed of straw was making him crazy. "Shall we see to the horses?" he asked instead. "Nice wellingtons," he added noting the knee-high rubber boots she wore as they worked together to bed down the horses.

"Turns out Evelyn and I are the same size."

"Really," said Chas, opening the door for her. "Too bad she doesn't ride."

Sam gave him a playful punch on the arm and they strolled in companionable silence back to the house.

As the morning light filled her bedroom, Sam rolled over with unaccustomed luxury, stretched and yawned. Her bottom might be tender from yesterday's fall in the mud, but it was nothing compared to the pains in her legs. And she'd thought she was in good shape, walking around

London's parks on the weekends, and getting off the underground ahead of her stop when the weather was nice. If she wanted to continue riding Max, she would have to up her game.

At least, she'd slept much better, despite knowing that, for her, every minute she spent in Chas' company would be fraught with danger. There was no denying his touch thrilled her, his kisses aroused her, and his playful courtship and backtrack towards friendship had impressed her. To be so close to falling in love, and then having to pretend it never happened, was going to be a challenge.

Don't think about it, she scolded herself; you've got work to do.

In fact, she was looking forward to the day, not just because of Chas, but because he was offering her a chance to pore over the treasures at Porter Hall. And that was like catnip to an antique specialist like her. Really, it was amazing. A few days ago, Chas could have presided over a board meeting without either of them giving each other a second look. His reserve ran deep and his employees respected his privacy. Sadly, it also meant they had never seen his vulnerable side, or the way his ice-blue eyes softened when he was aroused. At least, she hoped they hadn't. That particular pleasure had been all hers. And she'd like it to stay that way. Forever.

Enough daydreaming. She really should get up.

A discreet knock on the door ended her procrastination. The doorknob turned and in walked Evelyn Weekes carrying the now-familiar silver tray.

"Chas thought another morning with breakfast in bed was in order."

Sam struggled into a sitting position. "I could get used to this you know, and then where would you be."

"Down in the kitchen watching your breakfast get cold." The woman smiled.

"Touché," said Sam stretching out her arms to receive the tray. Like yesterday, the housekeeper had come bearing gifts. "I see my jeans under your arm, all clean and ready for another fun-filled day in the country, but what else have you brought?" Sam asked suspiciously. "Not more hand-me-downs, I hope."

"Oh, I suspect you'll like these ones," said the housekeeper setting a pile of men's shirts on the end of the bed. "They belong to Chas. He thought they'd be more suitable than, and I quote 'a suitcase full of little black dresses.'" She put her hands on her hips. "Nuff said."

Sam snorted. "Men have no idea. And he's waiting where?"

"In the library. Been hauling boxes back-and-forth for an hour now."

Shaking her head at life's mysteries, the housekeeper left the room. As soon as the door snugged shut, Sam set her breakfast to one side, and drew the pile of shirts towards her. Most were light blue, button-down and long sleeved. She fingered the soft cotton marvelling at her boss's thoughtfulness.

She put the shirts back down, but found she could barely take her eyes off them. If the gang at Burton-Porter & Sons ever caught wind of the special treatment she was receiving, they'd be aghast. For more reasons than one, Sam realized. She poured herself a cup of tea, plastered her croissant with butter and damson jam and ate like it was Christmas morning.

She slipped out of bed and padded across the room. It was only after her chat with Chas at the stables, that she'd come to realize how badly she wanted to stay at Porter Hall. As soon as she'd returned to her room, she'd emptied her suitcases. Her clothes were now in the armoire, her toiletries in the cabinet, and with the candlestick on the dresser, she felt at home.

It was odd really, how comfortable she felt at Porter Hall, thought Sam as she brushed her hair, now that she and Chas had come to an agreement. Even having Evelyn Weekes fuss over her seemed somehow acceptable. Sam paused mid-stroke, trying to work it out. She usually guarded her privacy. Maybe, she thought as she resumed her brushing, it was because the housekeeper was a calm and friendly presence. It was a nice change.

Sam laid her brush on the table and set about deciding what to wear...

...Holding out her shirttails with her fingertips, she did a little pirouette in front of the mirror, and then bowed to her reflection. Her grandmother would have said she was "do-lally" dancing about in her leggings, and ballerina flats. But what she really was, Sam decided, was happy. Unfortunately, she couldn't share it with anyone else.

Chas rubbed his temples while he waited. A couple of late-night scotches had kept his mind off Sam while he organized the files they'd need to catalogue the estate, but they'd done nothing to help him sleep. If anything they'd added fire to the flame and he'd woken with a splitting headache that even Evelyn's extra strong coffee couldn't cure.

A discreet clearing of the throat alerted him to Sam's presence. "Come in." He got to his feet carefully. Despite his dark mood, he couldn't deny the rush of warmth he felt seeing Sam in one of his old school shirts. "You're looking very elegant this morning, Miss Redfern."

"Thank you." She acknowledged the compliment, her voice so cool and composed they might as well have been in the showrooms at Burton-Porter.

All of which was fine with him.

"I thought we'd make the library our headquarters," said Chas drawing another chair up beside his own. "Cushion?" he asked, holding up a needlepoint pillow. At Sam's nod, he positioned it on the seat for her. They were back in the safe and comfortable world of work. He had his laptop open at one end of the oak table and when she had arrived, he had just begun to pour over the haphazard collection of documents they would need for listing the items he considered saleable when she arrived.

Keeping his tone guarded, Chas asked how she was feeling.

"Tender, but fine," said Sam, gingerly lowering herself into the chair. She did her best to make her answering smile nothing more than a polite acknowledgement, but oh how she wanted to lean in toward him, casually touch the strong forearm that was pulling the files closer to her. She wanted those wonderfully sensitive fingers to smooth across her aching back and shoulders, easing away the knots in her muscles as they untangled the knots in her emotions. Instead she leaned back, flipped open the notebook she carried and looked at Chas calmly.

Chas fought the impulse to slide his chair closer to Sam. The distance between them felt wrong, but it was necessary. In a few days, they would be heading back to the reality of London and their careers. She would remain the perfect Burton-Porter agent and, assuming there were no other disasters ahead of them, resume her personal life. It occurred to him then, that he had no idea about her personal life. Was there a boyfriend? He fought down a surge of jealousy. There couldn't be a lover or she would never have kissed him the way she did – there was too much honesty in those green eyes to be playing fast and loose with anyone…and besides he told himself ruthlessly, it was none of his business if she had ten lovers. She was his employee, his valued employee. Nothing more. Once they returned to the city, he would reclaim his solitary existence, invite a suitable woman out to dine and forget all about Samantha Redfern.

The idea was utterly depressing. It would be nigh impossible to forget Sam. Her very scent was enough to have him quivering with desire. No other woman had ever affected him this way. He shifted in his seat. He should be furious with her, not lusting after her.

"So where do we start?" Sam asked.

Her business-like manner ended his flight of fancy. He handed her a copy of the original architect's drawing of the manor and a family tree. He spoke while she scanned the documents. "There are three reception rooms, a study, library, and conservatory, six principle bedrooms and a warren of storerooms. After that we begin on the record books, loose receipts and an itemized list from my grandfather's estate." He gestured toward the dusty stack of folders and documents spread out on the table. "Inheritance taxes changed everything. And cost the estate a fortune." Not to mention his grandfather's inept handling of the land and philandering ways. "A lot of the best art was sold off. The smaller holdings were sold to tenants who could afford them. And needed repairs were left undone. Which explains these," he said pulling a half-dozen old ledgers towards them. "The account books track paintings sold and what was hung in their place."

Sam blinked. "Wouldn't someone from the art department be a better choice?"

Chas shook his head. "Only if we go to auction. Until then, it doesn't matter if they're fakes or not. Besides, from the First World War on, the estate records are less than meticulous. We have to sort out what we can."

"And the family portraits?"

"The best ones are down in London. No doubt you've seen them lining the halls of Burton-Porter glowering down at the staff."

"I thought I recognized that look."

He shot her a quelling glance. "You're teasing me, right?"

She grinned. "And the portraits here?" She gestured to a dark painting in an even darker corner of the library.

"That's one of our tasks – identifying the ones without much documentation. Quite a few were unearthed from the attic to cover the empty spots on the wall. Faded wallpaper is a great giveaway. And there you have it," said Chas getting to his feet. He held out the chair for Sam. "Will you be okay on your own?" he asked.

"Absolutely." Even though she was moving slowly, her eyes sparkled. "This is proving to be the most excellent adventure." He rather hoped she meant being with him, but he knew better than to discount the impact his wealth had on the opposite sex. He watched Sam gather her notes. If he was reading her correctly, she was as excited about him as she was about the job at hand. He should be pleased, Chas reminded himself, but he'd seen the passion lurking beneath the surface and he wanted more of it.

After a dizzying morning of foxes, hounds and horses, punctuated by the odd landscape, Sam found herself in a little used reception room on the second floor staring into the stern eyes of a dour woman wearing the dark finery of the late 19th-century. This old girl was definitely a Porter. She peered at Sam through hooded eyes, punctuated by a familiar hawk-like nose.

Sam shivered. Chas was lucky. On him, those harsh features were an enhancement. They made him look strong and commanding, and virile.

"Boo!"

Sam whirled around to see her boss standing directly behind her! "You scared me," she charged.

"Sorry about that," grinned Chas. "But I'm not surprised. You looked as though you'd fallen under the spell of Agnes the miserable, the elder sister of my great-great uncle. Direct action was required."

"She is rather...austere," said Sam.

"When my grandmother arrived at the Hall, she took one look at the portrait, and banished

Aunt Agnes to the attic where she languished for," Chas shrugged, "sixty years or more."

Sam nodded in heartfelt agreement. "I can see why your grandmother packed poor Agnes away. The question is why bring her out again?"

Chas grimaced. "Even the best of families get down to the dregs when money's tight. In our case, it was Aunt Agnes. A bad artist and a sour expression are a deadly combination, don't you think?"

"I can't argue with that." Sam turned to smile at Chas, feeling the heat of attraction once again. Even the baleful glare of his ancestor couldn't dim the flare of feeling she had for this man. Their eyes met and the moment stretched.

With a slight jerk, Chas stepped away. "Lunch in an hour?"

"Perfect." Despite her resolve to be professional, Sam's body rebelled. She watched him walk the length of the gallery, shamelessly ogling his muscular physique from head to toe, taking care to note how the tailor-made, fawn-coloured trousers accentuated his trim waist and perfect backside. Mia would be so proud of her, thought Sam. She knew her office buddy thought she was a prude, but here she was with her eyes glued to her boss's behind. And what a behind.

As Chas neared the end of the gallery, Sam quickly switched her concentration back to Aunt Agnes and started scribbling in her notebook. A good thing as she saw him look back briefly out of the corner of her eye before he disappeared from sight. Sam checked her watch. Fifty-five minutes and they'd be together again.

"Pull yourself together, Sam," she muttered. "Next thing you know you'll be talking to Aunt Agnes." She raised her eyes to the portrait. "I guess I already am." The elderly woman stared down at her, in sympathy or in admonishment, Sam couldn't decide. Perhaps she, too, had lusted after a man like Chas in her youth, maybe even stolen a kiss by the stream as she and Chas had when Max and Damien had sent them both tumbling into the mud. Even now, beneath the condescending gaze of Chas' great-great aunt, all Sam could think about was the feel of Chas' lips on hers and the warm weight of his body as he lay on top of her. She shuddered. "You probably don't approve of me, do you, Aunt Agnes?"

Sam got nothing in return but a haughty stare.

Confirming what she already knew. Every woman she had ever seen at her boss' side had screamed money and breeding. "I guess I wouldn't cut it in his world anyway," she told the portrait. At least, she consoled herself as she jotted down Aunt Agnes' particulars, she'd had a nibble from a former colleague at Sotheby's a few weeks back. He'd strongly suggested that if England didn't work out for her, she would be more than welcome in New York City. It wouldn't be difficult to slip back into her former life, thought Sam, but the funny thing was she'd rather be in Derbyshire talking to Chas' long-dead relatives.

By the third day, they had settled into a well-established routine. Breakfast on the terrace if the weather was warm enough, and then off to work. With Chas concentrating on furniture and the family's private quarters, they were often in separate parts of the Hall. But by mid-morning, they would reconvene in the library for coffee and to compare notes. It felt a bit like a treasure hunt to Sam as they cross-referenced their finds with the old, and often incomplete, handwritten records.

Lunch, then back to work with Evelyn Weekes reappearing around four with tea and biscuits. Her thoughtfulness was touching. "I like the company," she confided to Sam one afternoon. "Porter Hall comes alive when he's here…" And so she baked him Bakewell tarts and lemon cake and beamed with pleasure when the plate came back empty.

Neither of them mentioned going back to the city.

At the end of each afternoon, Chas would push himself back from the desk and say, "shall we head for the stables?" and Sam would race upstairs to change. She cherished these off-duty moments. Chas would boost her into the saddle and while she fought down the pure joy of his nearness, he would give her pointers on how to improve her natural skills. She still winced over the boots, but kept it to herself. It was a small price to pay for the thrill of his touch every time he repositioned her hands, or her legs, or adjusted the stirrups. From time to time, Sam had the sense that something serious was troubling him, but she knew better than to invade his privacy.

"Are you up for a real-life hurdle?" Chas asked late Wednesday afternoon. He had just coached Sam through a series of practice jumps and there was still a lot of light left in the day. When Sam nodded, he swung up on Damien's back. "We could ride across a different part of the estate. I'd like to check the upper fields. See if they're suitable for grazing."

Hiding her flash of anxiety over the prospect of another tumble, Sam readily agreed. What Chas had taught her was designed to increase her confidence. And she didn't intend to let either of them down with a sudden case of nerves.

"Lead on," she smiled brightly.

As they cantered along the edge of yet another sheep-filled pasture, Sam wrinkled her nose. Their musky smell was overwhelming sometimes. And then she caught sight of the new lambs. Her heart melted as she watched them struggle to find a foothold close to their mothers. The combination of their soft bawling and the thud of the horses' hooves was a perfect moment. Chas glanced over to see how she was doing and then held her gaze as they shared the warmth of the scene before them. It was, Sam thought, a moment of pure bliss.

At the end of the pasture, a low stone wall blocked their path. Chas urged Damien forward and effortlessly sailed over the fence. He guided the huge chestnut back around and stood waiting for Sam.

"All right?" he called.

Sam's answer was to kick Max forward. And then suddenly she was soaring, her body leaning into the jump, one with the horse as Max took flight over the stone wall. They landed perfectly, the jar so slight that Sam barely felt it.

She drew up beside Chas, her face beaming with pride. "You're a good teacher," she told him, "and you…" she bent down to pat Max's long neck, "are a champion."

When she looked up she saw that Chas' eyes were smouldering with heat. The air seemed to swirl around them as they gazed at each other in silence. Birds sang in the background, the horses bent their heads to the grass, but Sam and Chas were oblivious, locked in an emotional embrace that ignored the chasm between them.

Then Damien shook his massive head and broke the spell. "We should be going," said Chas. All Sam could do was nod. Her resolve was obviously not as strong as his. Disappointment seemed to go hand-in-hand with hope. Did he regret his openness of a few moments ago, or had his natural wariness caused him to draw back at the last minute.

She sighed. It was all part of the mystery that was Chas Porter.

They rode in single file hugging the edge of the field. Wildflowers bloomed amidst the tall grass and birds were busy building their nests in the branches of an old apple tree, chirping as they flew back and forth with tiny sticks, all of which Sam saw, but didn't register. Her heart was in a knot. Beyond the tree, she could see that the stones had crumbled away, leaving a wide break in the wall. Chas paused as if he were making a mental note to have it repaired and then they passed through to the meadow leading back to the house.

"Ready for a gallop?" asked Chas turning in the saddle. He had reverted to the carefully guarded tone he had adopted after their falling out by the stream.

She tried to read his eyes, but to no avail. Whatever turmoil he was going through presumably mirrored her own. She needed to be as kind and understanding as he had been with her, but tell that to the constant thrum of longing she felt whenever he was near.

"Let's go," she said urging Max forward until he was neck and neck with Damien. The rush of wind lifted Sam's spirits and she flashed Chas a brilliant smile. Enjoying the moment was the secret to life, she decided, not agonizing over what could and could not be. Had she not slammed into Chas at the auction, she would have been trudging the streets of New York.

By the time they reached the stable, Sam's cheeks were flushed with colour. She was ready in equal parts for both a shower and dinner, but the horses had to be seen to first. Stick to routine, she told herself, you can think about the way Chas had savoured you with his eyes at a later date. Right now, she needed to walk Max around the yard to cool them both down. Being desirable was a good thing, she decided, but honestly, she could scream with frustration.

Just then John Weekes appeared in the stable yard to interrupt her thoughts.

"I'll take care of the horses," he announced to Chas who was over by the mounting block removing a clump of mud from Damien's back hoof. "The wife has your supper near ready and she says you've just time to clean up before it spoils."

"Excellent," said Chas lowering Damien's leg to the ground. "Sam? Would you pass Max over to John?"

Gratefully, Sam relinquished the reins with a murmur of thanks and unclipped her helmet. While Chas described the break in the wall to John Weekes, Sam headed for the tack room. She ran her fingers through her damp hair as she walked, relishing the cool breeze against her skin.

Stepping inside the stable, she felt a pang of loss. Sooner or later, she would be leaving Porter Hall. If she stayed at Burton-Porter & Sons, she would still see Chas, but there would be no more afternoon rides, no more Max, and no more Damien. Walking past the empty stalls, she realized just how attached she had become to everyone, and everything at the Hall. Evelyn Weekes couldn't have been more welcoming, and Chas…despite their rough beginning, had been a wonderful host.

She had barely reached the tack room when she heard him come in behind her. They set their helmets down on the shelf. Then, without a word, Chas took her by the arm and spun her around. He cupped her face in his hands and gazed down at her. "Don't ever mistake my reticence for anything but respect, Sam."

His hooded eyes bored into her very being as he lowered his face, his lips seeking hers with a surety of purpose. No more denial, no more disciplined retreat, nor more distance between them. She was his to plunder.

Only the opening of the stable door and the clip-clopping of hooves drew them apart. "We're not finished you and I," growled Chas as he stepped back. His eyes raked her from head to toe and Sam heard herself groan in response. "You go ahead," he said abruptly, "John's no fool."

Sam was lost in space when Chas returned to the terrace with a tray of after-dinner drinks. "Sorry to take so long," he shook his head. "I had another phone call from London."

"Here," said Sam, rising from her chair, "let me take that." She reached for the tray, careful not to brush his fingers with hers. Every time they "accidentally" connected, a jolt of electricity would race through her body, a tantalizing reminder of how perfectly suited they were. If she weren't careful, they would be right back where they started from, although after their brief encounter in the tack room, she wasn't sure they would be able to maintain the delicate balance of their relationship much longer.

Seated again, with a glass of wine in her hand, Sam stole a glance at her boss and found his blue eyes watching her over the rim of his glass. Did he feel the same way, she wondered as she sipped her wine, and did that explain why he hadn't made a move to rekindle the passion they'd felt from the beginning before now? She was sure it had begun before they'd even left the auction hall. In fact, from the moment she'd run smack into him with the candlestick pressed between her breasts, she'd been drawn to him like a moth to a flame.

Had she not postponed her trip to New York so she could attend the auction, she would never have known Chas Porter for the man he really was, nor seen this magnificent estate and come to learn more about his family history. She shivered; it was all worth it, not matter how they parted. She blinked and quickly averted her gaze. The thought of their relationship, however unusual, coming to an end was beyond thinking about. But sooner or later, as sure as spring turned to summer, it would. London was already beckoning.

Best shove it to the back of her mind and enjoy whatever time they had together.

"I have to go into the city tomorrow, drop the car off at the dealership," Chas announced after downing the rest of his whiskey "and meet with a couple of our biggest clients who need reassuring." His expression darkened. "Apparently one of our competitors is trying to entice them away with a rumour that we're in financial difficulty."

"But why…" she began.

"Because we're down here cataloguing the estate."

Sam rubbed her forehead. She hadn't spoken to anyone at the office in nearly a week. "I don't understand," she said.

"If Porter Hall comes on the market, people will wonder why."

"But it's not about the money…" Sam frowned. "Can't you…" Her voice trailed away. The irony was, Chas was so much happier at Porter Hall than she'd ever seen him in London, it didn't make sense for him to sell unless…

"Sam!" Chas cut into her thoughts. "Don't worry about it. It's not as though I haven't been here before. When I inherited, there were dealers up and down the country expecting me to fail." He picked up his glass. "How about a toast to Burton-Porter & Sons?"

"To Burton-Porter & Sons," said Sam, clinking her glass against his.

From there, they chatted about everyday things, told a couple of funny stories from their childhoods, and admired the view, bathed in the softening light of a spectacular sunset.

"I don't ever remember the weather being this consistently beautiful," breathed Chas, "it's been perfect." He was reaching for her hand when his mobile went off, destroying the moment. Chas picked it up and checked the call display. His eyebrows snapped together. Standing, he nodded to Sam.

"Sorry," he said, "I won't be long."

She sighed.

Now that the sky had lost its colour, she felt chilled. She should go inside, she decided. There was always more to do. She picked up the tray and took it inside with her, setting it down in the library, while she reviewed today's inventory. Chas had said he was satisfied with their progress on the artwork and the library. But much of that progress had to do with his intimate knowledge of the wealth he'd grown up with. Tomorrow, he would be in London and she would be on her own. With the silver collection.

Suddenly anxious that there might be questions she needed to ask, Sam turned to the ledgers which itemized the collection. The once extensive silver had obviously meant easy cash to the previous owners. Much had been sold or simply disappeared from the books. Sam's brows knit as she tried to puzzle out whether she was looking at just bad bookkeeping or if someone had deliberately made off with the family silver. It didn't make sense. Just as Chas' insistent bidding on that single silver candlestick didn't make sense.

She closed the ledger and pushed back her chair.

He'd given her carte-blanche from day one. Why should the locked silver cabinet be any different?

The dining room was as it had been on their first evening at the Hall. Goose bumps ran up and down her arms when she remembered tiptoeing into the room wearing nothing but a thin nightgown beneath her shawl. Their first kiss. She could almost feel the key pressing against her back when he'd leaned in to take his first taste of her.

Crossing the room to the silver cabinet, she stopped cold. The key was gone. Her forehead creased in a frown. Had Chas removed it? What was going on here? What had seemed to be a simple inventory was taking on undercurrents that put her on edge. She put her fingers into the handles and jiggled the door. Yes, it was thoroughly locked.

Mild irritation began to rise into anger. *Deep breath, Sam*, she whispered. *Just because you have a history with this silver, doesn't mean that Chas does.*

Stepping closer to jiggle the door again, her foot caught something just under the lip of the cabinet. The key. It had simply fallen from the lock. Chas had not been trying to hide something from her.

Feeling foolish, she stood up and slid the key into the lock, turned it, pulled open its beautifully crafted doors, and then gasped. There, sitting boldly at the front, stood ten exquisite silver George II candlesticks. Identical to the one she had just purchased. Identical to the one she had inherited from her grandparents.

Anger and confusion welled from some place deep within her, pounding through her veins, roaring through her head into a tidal wave of rage.

At that moment, Chas entered the room.

He scowled. "I see you've gotten ahead of me," he bristled.

"It's about time," Sam snapped, "as I've apparently been behind you up until now." She pointed to the candlesticks. "You've been lying to me," she said flatly. "Did you plan to remove them before I saw the rest of the silver collection?"

"No, of course not," Chas said. "Let me explain…"

"I don't want explanations," Sam cried out. "You tricked me! You tricked me into coming here, you tricked me into falling for you, and now…this!"

Chas' eyes hardened. "I've been trying to put things right," he seethed. "Trying to repair what my father and grandfather destroyed. I admit I should have told you why I needed you here. Why I need an expert to authenticate what I'm not sure of."

Sam stood her ground, eyes glittering with unshed tears. "Well you got what you wanted, Mr.

Porter," she spat out. "And everything else, was that just part of keeping your expert on hand? I can't believe how stupid I've been. I actually thought there was a real friendship growing between us, a real…" her voice suddenly gave out.

She turned, brushed past Chas and strode out of the room, back straight, tears held back. Until she reached her room. Then, despite her best resolve, she got into bed, and using the pillows to muffle her sobs, wept until there wasn't a tear left in her.

Seven

The sound of a car engine roused Sam from yet another restless dream. A quick check of the time told her it was two-fifteen. Concerned, she slipped out of bed and ran across to the window seat just in time to see a pair of headlights clip the corner of the coach house and disappear from view.

It had to be Chas. On his way back to London, choosing to drive through the night rather than face her in the morning. It was her own fault, she thought. They were supposed to be friends, but she had flung accusations and locked herself in her room, not giving him even a moment to explain. But was there really an explanation, beyond the obvious?

Her heart sank.

She was alone in the house, the granddaughter of a housemaid and a groom sleeping in a bedroom not unlike one her Gran might have cleaned. Crawling back into bed, Sam drew the covers over her head, but that didn't stop her mind whirling through the possibilities that had plagued her since she had opened the cabinet to see Chas' silver collection. She'd known since she was a little girl not to pester her grandparents about the candlestick and how they'd come to own it. But if they had been in service, how could they have afforded such an expensive piece? As honest as the day was long, Sam knew they would never have stolen it no matter how badly they might have been treated by their former employers.

And, knowing the risks she had taken to obtain its match, why hadn't Chas told her he already had ten identical candlesticks? What was the secret behind these pieces of silver? Sam felt like she was blundering about in a darkened room, playing blind man's bluff with Chas.

He'd betrayed her trust, she decided. Just as she had his. Funny thing, betrayal. It came in all shapes and sizes and just when you forgot it existed, it threw you a curve ball. Which landed in the pit of your stomach. And had you revisiting every moment, every kiss, and every endearment looking for hidden meanings. Would they have been better off if they'd been open with each other from the beginning?

She didn't know.

And now she was worried sick about Chas making his way down to London, likely without sleep and with unresolved issues between them. Odd that they were so alike. Advance, retreat, reveal, hide. He was probably as angry with himself as he was with her.

And there was nothing she could do about it.

Tugging the duvet over her shoulder as she rolled, Sam burrowed beneath the covers and curled into a ball. Mercifully, her fatigue won over and she fell into a fitful sleep. When she raised her head from the pillow a few hours later, the sky had changed from pitch black to a predawn grey, way too early for a city girl like her. Lying on her back, she stared at the ceiling feeling sorry for herself. A luxury she could not afford. She needed to get up and get started. She would catalogue the silver, every single piece of it. Maybe when she'd finished she would be able to make sense of Chas' behaviour the night before.

By early afternoon, Sam was back in the library scanning her notes and merging them with the files already on the computer. The sterling silver flatware tallied with her master list as did the plethora of serving dishes, the three Georgian tea services, six massive candelabras and a hideous epergne, all of which were stored in the butler's pantry. She'd already logged most of the other silver about the Hall, the snuffboxes in the drawing room, and the coasters in the reception rooms and inkwells in Chas' study. Obviously the Burton-Porters had been avid collectors, yet the original inventory, she noted, did not list the candlesticks; surely if they'd been family pieces, they would have been included with Randolph Porter's other assets.

Frowning, Sam leaned back in her chair. The candlesticks were made about the same time

Porter Hall was built in the mid-18th century which meant, conceivably, they could have been original to the house. But that didn't fit with what Chas had told her. Why did it matter so much? Why did she want so badly to be able to completely trust him, no matter what the lists and ledgers showed? So leave it alone, she scolded herself. Hadn't he given her the benefit of the doubt when she'd been less than honest with him? That brought the memory of the first time she had stumbled and leaned on that broad chest of his. All that strength had seared through her skin into her being.

Just when her memories were getting a bit too heated for comfort, Sam sensed she was no longer alone. Evelyn Weekes hovered in the open doorway, holding up a portable phone. "You have a call from London," she announced stepping into the room.

"Really?" Sam lurched from her chair, her hand already reaching to snatch the phone from the older woman's hand.

As soon as she had it, Sam said her thanks. And with heart thumping, raised the handset to her ear. "Hello?" she said. .

"Sam!" A familiar voice screeched down the line. "Is that really you?"

Definitely not Chas.

"Mia," said Sam, trying to hide her disappointment as the housekeeper discreetly closed the library door behind her. "How are you?"

"Other than worrying about you, I'm fine. Are you in a dead zone, or what?"

Sam blinked. Being at Porter Hall was like being in never-never land. When she couldn't find a signal the first night, she'd convinced herself there was no service. She didn't need to answer her phone or check her messages. Partly, she had to acknowledge, because she was ashamed and embarrassed by her own actions. After rescheduling her flight to New York, not telling anybody about her change in plans, and then ending up at Porter Hall to help the head of the company do a private inventory of his estate, tongues would be wagging and questions would be asked. Thank goodness, they didn't know she'd used her expense money to cover her purchase at the auction hall. And, they never would. Even though she had acted unethically, Sam knew Chas would never mention it to anyone else.

"The reception here is hit-and-miss," she said finally. She squeezed her eyes shut and waited for Mia to tell her what had happened at Burton-Porter & Sons in her absence. If Mia felt free to call Porter Hall, that meant Chas was safe and sound and in London.

"I think you were too distracted to check," drawled Mia.

That was an understatement, thought Sam. In five short days, her heart had been through the wringer and back again. But what to say? I think I'm in love with the boss? Or, how about I'm pathetically grateful not to be in jail for fraud? There was nothing really she could say without further jeopardizing her reputation or her relationship with Chas. "Cataloguing an estate takes time."

"Is that what you call it?" said Mia.

"Not funny. How did you get this number?" demanded Sam. Company policy guaranteed privacy both for their clients and their staff. No one gave out that information without first clearing it with those involved.

"I was roller-blading through the back hallway this morning as per usual, and there he was…just coming out of the staff room with a cup of coffee like a normal guy… I damn near ran him down and all he did was smile at me and say 'Hello, Mia'. Sam…what have you done to the man? He's being weirdly…nice."

Probably relief that he'd left his most troublesome employee behind, thought Sam sourly.

"I asked him how you were," Mia's voice bubbled over with excitement, "and he gave me the number. Just like that. I could hardly believe it." They nattered for a few minutes about this-and-that; all the while Sam's mind was racing.

"Did he say anything else?"

"Well, he did ask me if I'd solved the glitch in our accounting system…"

"You know damn well what I mean, Mia."

"Fine. He wanted me to let you know that he was in the office and that if you needed anything, anything at all…'you were to call him personally'."

As Mia paused hopefully, relief flooded Sam's body. Chas was okay, at the very least they were still colleagues, and for once, her friend wasn't ragging her. Which could only mean one thing. Sam's eyes narrowed. Mia knew something was up between them. Sam had been with Chas for the better part of the week. The estate they were cataloguing was indeed Porter Hall and now the man more commonly known as Chas "bloody" Porter had revealed himself to be a nice guy.

The Burton-Porter grapevine must be buzzing with speculation!

Sam sat down with a thump. "Mia…" she quizzed, "what's everyone been saying?"

"Ahh, now that's the interesting part. The guys down at the warehouse are running a pool. It's currently four to one that the next family portrait will have green eyes. I can spot you five pounds if you wanna place a bet?"

"Mia!" she croaked into the phone. At which point, Mia burst into a chorus of "New York, New York," before laughing uproariously and hanging up.

Sam set the phone down and covered her mouth with her hand. They were the hottest topic of office gossip. She didn't know whether to laugh or cry. Chas would be furious, but she was thrilled! At least, her girlie side was, thanks to the goddess of single women. But where did that leave

Sam when they returned to London? Would her "friend" Chas who occupied more and more of her thoughts, turn back into her cold, distant boss? Or did the man she rode with, laughed with, and sparred with still exist in the city? If she was the subject of gossip and Chas had had enough, would a sophisticated, professional reason be found to dump her out of the office on her embarrassing keester?

Sam's eyes widened. She'd been so involved with Chas, she'd totally forgotten about her Sotheby's contact. They'd been scheduled to have lunch together when she was in New York and talk about a position opening up at one of the major houses that would be perfect for her. With a sense of panic she realized that if her relationship with Chas didn't include either a professional or personal happily ever after, she would need that job.

Racing upstairs, Sam grabbed her purse and dug out her mobile. As soon as she turned on the power, scads of texts and emails began to download. Her inbox was jammed. Ignoring all the messages from Mia and co-workers, she opened an email from New York. "Sorry you couldn't make the trip, but the offer still stands. Head of the silver department is yours for the taking."

Stunned, Sam plonked herself down on the side of the bed.

She would have to decide by the end of the month. She sent a quick note of acknowledgement and then turned off her phone. Her head was aching. Random thoughts of the "what if" variety ricocheted like pinballs. If she jumped at the opportunity to return to New York and it didn't work out, she would have closed the door on Burton-Porter forever. If she listened to her heart, she would never leave England…unless said heart was broken.

Sam gripped her phone in both hands and stared across the room at a particularly beautiful landscape. In despair she realized that Porter Hall was her perfect landscape – with the focal point her tall, handsome and attractively brooding boss.

"Samantha Redfern," she told herself sternly, "you are an idiot who needs to stop daydreaming and start getting practical." But when was love ever practical?

Mia had said Chas was like a bull in a china shop when he wasn't grinning from ear-to-ear, as though he'd forgotten his London cloak of cool indifference. What that exactly meant, Sam had no idea. Maybe he was just happy to be back in the city. Maybe one of those perfect women who usually hung on his arm had already reminded him of the pleasures of the single, sophisticated state.

But that shouldn't bother her, Sam told herself glumly. This is just a job and the boss was just amusing himself as bosses do. Never mind that Chas had a reputation for treating his employees with intense integrity. Maybe, Sam thought, when she'd used company funds to buy the candlestick she'd declared the integrity clause null and void between them.

This biting loneliness and the ridiculous way she missed Chas, she had brought onto herself. And if nothing else, she had better show that she could at least do a superb job at the task she had been hired for by Burton-Porter.

Scolding herself for mooning about when she could be working, Sam shoved her mobile back in her bag and tripped down the main staircase. In the library, she surveyed the neat stack of folders awaiting her and sighed. She had been working for more than six hours already, and she needed a better break than Mia's phone call had provided. Collecting her coffee cup, Sam wandered past the smaller, family dining room where they ate on chilly days and headed down to the warmth of the big kitchen.

Evelyn Weekes was at the counter chopping carrots for a casserole. "Finished for the day?" she asked Sam.

"Just for the time being," said Sam setting her mug on the counter. "I might get back to it later." She sneezed. "Sorry. I guess the dust is getting to me." Too late, she saw the housekeeper's back stiffen and then relax when Sam said. "Old books are so dry they can crumble like fallen leaves if you're not careful."

The housekeeper chortled. "I knew you couldn't be referring to my housecleaning." She picked up the cutting board and slid the carrots into the pot with the edge of her knife. "Cup of tea?" she asked wiping her hands on a towel when she was finished.

"Only if you'll join me," said Sam.

"Don't mind if I do."

While the older woman set about making a pot of tea, Sam's thoughts drifted. To the silver collection and what Chas wasn't telling her, to the mystery behind the candlestick owned by her grandparents and now residing in her London flat, and to how much she missed being with Chas. There had to be some way to figure out what the connection was between the candlesticks. Somewhere there must be records she had not yet examined. She was itching to ask the housekeeper if she knew where the estate papers would be, but that would put the woman in an awkward position.

A shaft of sunlight carved a path across the kitchen table. Maybe a dose of fresh air and sunshine was what she needed. "Evelyn," said Sam. "May I ask you a question…about the rose garden?"

"Now that's a sad story," said the housekeeper. She untied her apron and hung it up on a peg by the back door. "Why don't we take our tea outside?" she suggested. With Sam's help they set the tray and carried it outside to the terrace, settling at one of the wrought iron tables that overlooked the gardens. "When I first came to the Hall," the housekeeper continued over tea, "it was magnificent out here. I used to go along this terrace whenever I could just to smell the roses. Mrs. Porter, that would be Sylvia, Chas' mother, oversaw the gardens. She wasn't that interested in gardening, but she did like to entertain. Weekend parties and the like. And everything had to be perfect." The housekeeper set her cup down. "It was Eugenie Porter, Chas' grandmother, who designed the beds and raised roses. Visitors used to come just to tour the gardens and look at the roses. A few were quite rare – she collected them from old gardens as the cities sprawled out and ate them up. Not so much is left of the gardens now, but John cares for the roses for the old lady's sake. And because I do love the scent." She smiled.

"Could we take a turn about the gardens?" asked Sam, her own tea finished.

"You go ahead, dear. I'll take in the tea tray."

A few minutes later, the housekeeper was back with a basket over her arm. "Care to join me in a bit of weeding?" she asked Sam. She held up a pair of gloves and a trowel. "It helps out John and we can chat while we work."

Sam joined in with enthusiasm. "This is a perfect way to end the afternoon." They worked their way along the beds lining the flagstone terrace. When she reached a mounded shrub, Sam paused to admire the greyish-green leaves and tight buds emerging from its thorny stems. All of a sudden, the hair at the nape of her neck began to prickle.

"This is a York and Lancaster damask, isn't it?"

"Now how on earth would you know that?" asked Evelyn pausing in mid-snip to gape at Sam. "Very few gardeners take the time for the old roses like this one. And I didn't take you for a muck-in-the-mud type."

"My grandmother," Sam stammered. As she leaned over to touch the rose's soft leaves, the poignancy of the fragrance to come filled her eyes with tears. "On Sundays," she paused to clear her throat, "we would take the streetcar to whichever rose garden was open to the public." Memories of her grandmother walking up and down the gravel paths clouded her thoughts. "Gran would stop to name the variety of every rose we passed and tell me its history until I could recite it back to her. Including….this one."

"This rose thrived. In Toronto?" The housekeeper frowned skeptically.

Sam laughed. "Don't worry, they're wrapped in burlap overcoats every winter."

"And did she have her own garden, your grandmother?" Evelyn pulled up another dandelion from the soft earth and added it to their pile.

"Just a vegetable patch," said Sam, resting on her knees, "with six hardy rose bushes, one at the end of each row so she could see them from the window. It was a little house," she added, "cozy and full of love."

"Just goes to show you," said the housekeeper, back to snipping unwanted stems, "it's about the people." She sniffed. "If my years at the Hall have taught me anything, it's love what makes a home, and there's not been much of that here at Porter Hall since the old lady died."

The two women worked in companionable silence, loosening the soil around the plants and tugging out the ubiquitous weeds, the garden's earthy perfume tugging at Sam's memory. Grace Quinn, always respectful of other people's property, would never have picked a rose, but if a petal happened to drop, she would snap it up, name it, smell it and fold it into her handkerchief. When they got home, she would add it the others she collected. "Roses are like family," she would say, "even dried, their scent lives on in your heart." And Sam knew her grandmother was thinking of her own daughter, Sam's mother, who had been at her side when she was a girl, learning the different names and collecting the petals just like Sam.

"Are you okay, dear?" asked the housekeeper.

Hearing her speak, Sam suddenly realized why she was so comfortable around Evelyn Weekes. It was her accent. Grace's voice had been softer, her accent less distinct, but the same clipped vowels that peppered Evelyn Weekes' speech had stayed with Grace until the day she died.

The rose, the candlestick, the Irish groom and now this.

She had to ask.

"Evelyn…?" Sam began…"Do you remember the house when it was fully staffed?"

"Before my time, dear…" The housekeeper sat back on her haunches. "Is there something specific you want to ask?"

"Not yet," said Sam.

"Well then, when you do, you might want to pay old George a visit down at the home farm. You've met George, have you?" At Sam's nod, the housekeeper continued, "his mother used to come up to the Hall when they had extra guests. That would be in the old lady's time. Whatever might still be known about those days, George would be the one to ask."

"Then I'll ride over to visit," Sam smiled.

"I'll make extra scones in the morning. You can take them for his tea," Evelyn said.

Sam nodded and returned to the weeding. She would ask him about his mother's days at the Hall and see where the conversation took them. At the very least, she would get out with Max. But she'd ride across the meadow – the path by the stream held too many memories.

With the staff gone for the day, Chas thought he'd be able to relax yet he couldn't seem to settle into his regular routine. The problem was obvious. He'd far rather be duking it out with Sam in Derbyshire than strutting around London in a suit and tie.

What was it about women; no, rephrase that, what was it about Sam? Her lush figure, her unexpectedly fiery temper, or her flashing green eyes that so captivated and beckoned him to step beyond his normal boundaries.

He loosened his tie and leaned back in his chair.

If the repairs to his car had been finished on time, he could have rescheduled his morning meetings and driven home tonight. But that was not to be. His eyes slid to the phone sitting on his desk. Perhaps, he should call Sam now and apologize.

He drummed his fingers on the arm of his chair.

She would be alone in the house.

Maybe nervous.

On the other hand, she might resent his call and misinterpret it as checking up on her. As if she'd run off with the silver. He grinned. Maybe she had. She'd been angry enough when she realized he'd been holding out on her.

His indecision was laughable, and made him think that his teenage years hadn't been so bad after all. He had never suffered from this ridiculous false bravado. Or the awkward hemming and hawing stage that seemed to plague other boys. He'd simply avoided the pain of dating. And then, once he'd become head of Burton-Porter & Sons, it had become so much easier; most women gravitated to money, power and prestige. Knowing that had allowed him to keep his distance. A stance he was finding harder and harder to maintain. Especially with Sam. She didn't give a hoot how much money he had, she would judge him by his behaviour, and already had on more than one occasion. Nor was she shy in pointing it out. Look at the way she had stood her ground at the auction hall and then again in the restaurant. It had been their first encounter away from Burton-Porter or any related function, and it made him realize how much of life he was missing.

He wondered what she was doing now. Was she still hard at work on the estate? Or had she turned off the computer and relaxed with a book? He pictured her curled up in one of the armchairs in the library, her porcelain skin radiant in the soft spill of light from the setting sun. Groaning audibly, Chas flicked his wrist to check the time, forgetting that in his haste to leave the Hall, he'd left his watch behind. Hopefully, it was in its usual spot in his room.

From there, it wasn't hard to envision Sam moving about his bedchamber, belonging there with him, responding to his touch as they shared their lives together. Her hair would be down, he decided, loose and luxurious, and glowing with health.

His fingers twitched with need.

Decision made, he practically snatched the phone from its cradle and dialed the Hall. Ten seconds later, he heard the answering burr. After five rings, Chas began to get concerned, after seven, he was worried.

Finally, Sam answered. "Hello?" She sounded out of breath.

"It's me," he said.

"Yes, it is." He could hear the laughter in her voice, and the knot in his stomach unclenched for the first time since he'd left the Hall.

"Are you busy?"

"As a matter of fact, I was up the ladder in the library trying to find a first edition of *Gulliver's Travels*. You don't happen to know where it is, do you?"

"Try the study." Chas put his feet up on his desk. "Under the atlas."

"Now why didn't I think of that?"

And so he found himself grinning down the line, like a fool in love, which, of course, he wasn't. Never had been, never wanted to be…

"So…how was your day? Everything go okay?" Even though he was never, ever going to be a fool in love, it seemed very important that her day had gone well. That she was content doing what she did best in his home.

"Perfect," replied Sam. "Inputting my notes went faster than I expected. Evelyn left a chicken casserole in the warming oven, which was delicious, and I finished the rest of that chardonnay. I hope that's okay."

"Of course. There should be another one in the wine fridge. In case you can't sleep or something…"

his sentence faltered. Mustn't think about sleep or imagine Sam snuggling into bed beside him. Desperately, he searched for a topic that was as far away from that particular fantasy as he could get. "I ran into your friend, Mia, this morning. Literally, I might add. Did she call?"

"Uh, huh." A note of caution crept into their conversation. He ploughed on, anxious to dispel Sam's concerns about his encounter with Mia and anything she might have said.

"Does she always roller blade to work...and at work?"

"Rain or shine," Sam was sounding bubbly again. "She's saving for a scooter."

"Ah," said Chas. "You're not going to tell me I don't pay her enough, are you?"

"Are you baiting me, Mr. Porter...?"

"Actually, I was trying to reassure you...look, Sam," he began, "I seem to be making a bad habit of this..." he took a deep breath, "but I am truly sorry about last night. I should have told you about the other candlesticks sooner..."

"...no, not really," replied Sam slowly. "Not after the auction. It was pretty awkward all round, as I'm sure you recall."

Chas frowned. She was letting him off way too easily. She had been stunned to see the candlesticks last night, stunned and furious, and then she'd clammed up. He'd assumed it was because he hadn't told her about the collection. Perhaps she'd guessed from the record's more recent entries that he was quietly trying to recover lost pieces, but why would that send her into such a state? Something was beginning to gnaw at the back of his mind, something unsettling, something he couldn't quite put his finger on…

Was there no end to the riddle that was Samantha Redfern?

"Does that mean you forgive me?" He injected a teasing note into his question, hoping she would not sense how ridiculously anxious he was to get back to their friendly, professional…no scratch that, their intimate, loving, and totally sensual relationship. Alone in his darkened office, he had been thinking of little else.

"Yes," answered Sam. "But, on one condition. That you forgive my outburst."

"If it means we're friends again, then yes."

"Deal," said Sam.

Chas let out an audible sigh of relief. "In that case…may I entice you upstairs, Miss Redfern? I…um, need a favour."

"Why, Mr. Porter…" came Sam's coquettish reply. "Whatever do you mean?"

Chas replied with a throaty chuckle. "I would like you to check my bedroom and see if my watch is where I left it, and not languishing in some rest stop on the way to London."

"That is the most pathetic come-on line I've ever heard."

"Hey, it was the best I could come up with on short notice…besides, it's true."

Sam laughed. "You'll have to give me directions." The pitch of her voice changed as she left the library and crossed the vestibule. "I don't know exactly where your bedroom is…not having been there before…"

"Ah…" They both paused, the silence between them laden with unspoken desires. "Left at the top of the stairs." Chas directed. "Third door on the right." He felt his pulse quicken. His image of Sam mounting the stairs and then silently gliding along the corridor as she approached his bedroom was bordering on the erotic.

Sam talked as she walked, giving Chas an update on what was left to do before she called it a day. He heard himself make the appropriate sounds of agreement, but he was definitely having trouble concentrating. "Are you listening to me?" Sam asked with a ripple of laughter, "or are you multitasking with a file of invoices on your desk?"

"Listening to you," Chas assured her. He heard the metallic click as she turned the handle of the door to his room. Chas' mouth went dry. She was there. The old brass hinges creaked slightly. And, then nothing.

Warily, Sam peeked inside. Even without the lights on, she could see Chas' imprint everywhere. She reached up and flicked the switch, illuminating the perfectly-proportioned room. Its beauty left her breathless.

"Oh, wow," Sam said softly. "I had no idea…"

"My one big indulgence at the Hall," she heard Chas say, "was to redecorate the master bedroom and make it my own."

"I'm impressed," said Sam, her shrewd eye assessing the natural look of the Belgian linens on the bed, the deep reds in the Persian rug on the floor. His palate was creamy white complimented by a deep red in the pillows and the armchairs flanking the fireplace. Like her room, only much larger, Chas' suite angled towards the woods, but his was sighted so that he could see the terrace below. Here, the window seat was deeper, more sumptuous, with room for two, thought Sam warming to the thought. She felt the flush in her cheeks as she pictured them together, arms entwined, sharing soft kisses as they watched the sun go down.

"Are you still there?" said a voice in her ear.

Sam dragged herself away from the scene she'd been watching in her head. "Just admiring your...furnishings." *And seeing myself sprawled across them.*

"...my watch?" Chas prompted.

"Right." Sam hurriedly panned the room, "any suggestions?"

"Try the bedside table."

"Which one?"

"The one on the right. I sleep on the right."

"Me, too." What on earth was she doing? Telling her boss what side of the bed she slept on while she prowled about his room, taking inventory, and soaking up his lingering scent as she went from one side of the bed to the other. His bedside table was a three-drawer chest. An angle poise lamp, a stack of books, an empty cut-glass tumbler, and next to it…an extremely expensive watch.

"Got it," said Sam.

"That's a relief," said Chas, "it was a gift from my grandmother."

"It's beautiful. May I?"

"Of course."

Sam picked up the watch. It was heavier than she expected. Elegant rather than fancy with a classic face. She sat down on Chas' bed and rubbed the silver chasing with the pad of her thumb. Like magic, all the complications between them simply slipped away.

"Where are you now?"

"On the edge of the bed. Sorry. I really should be going."

"Stay. Talk to me."

Sam felt her heart flip flop. She could hear Chas clear his throat on the other end of the line.

"How was work?" she asked, scrambling to get a handle on her own emotions.

"Other than the leering glances no one thought I would notice, it was extremely busy. The catalogue for the fall sales looks fantastic, and we'll be handling, with the utmost discretion, of course, the art collection of a major dealer."

"Brilliant. Are you in your office?"

"Jacket off, feet up and missing you like crazy."

"It's strange being here without you," said Sam. She lay back and stretched out on the bed, the watch still in the palm of her hand, warm and reassuringly male like the man who wore it. Against his skin. Most men never thought how sexy they could be, shirt sleeves rolled up to reveal muscular forearms and the promise of what lay hidden from view.

"I can see you lying there, with the firelight flickering over your face and hair."

Sam felt a shiver run down her spine and closed her eyes. "Made even better if you were here with me," she whispered. Her rising desire was palpable. She felt lithe and languorous, and entirely focused on the man on the other end of the line.

"Are you wearing another one of my shirts?" Chas asked her, his voice soft and low in her ear.

"Yes," said Sam. "My second of the day." She told him about her time outside with Evelyn Weekes tidying the rose garden while they enjoyed the afternoon sun. "Would you mind if I rode Max tomorrow," she asked, "and stopped in to see George?"

"I suppose…"

"You're not jealous of George, are you?" Sam teased.

"Actually, I was thinking of Max."

"I'll be riding him, it's Damien you should be thinking of…" Sam laughed. "Wait a minute now. Did I just set you up?"

"I don't know what…hold on, I hear footsteps." Chas' chair juddered as his weight shifted. "Guess I'm not alone in the building after all… Hey, Dave, how are you?" She heard him say in the background. The office security guard must be doing his rounds. "Five minutes, I should think. Yeah. Front entrance."

"I've been rousted." he breathed into the phone.

"I thought you owned the place?"

"I do. Unfortunately, that doesn't always make me the boss….anyway, let's not talk shop…"

"What would you like to talk about," Sam whispered. She wondered if he could hear her heart thumping. In her mind, she saw the intense look in his hooded eyes, the ripple of muscles as he stretched, relaxing into their conversation.

"I'd like to hold you," Chas replied, his voice dusky with desire. "All of you. I would like to get to know you in every way, Samantha Redfern. I want to know the feel of you, the taste of you. I want to feel the heat of your skin under my hands and hold you so close your breath melds with mine."

Sam's pulse quickened and she felt a quiver of fire in her belly. "I've wanted you ever since our first kiss." She knew what she was saying, the invitation she was offering. Even though every sensible particle in her brain told her this was not a good idea, the passion she felt for this man was deeper than any she had ever experienced.

Yet despite her words of love, she knew she wasn't ready. Her heart and soul could yearn for

Chas all they wanted, but until she knew exactly who she was and how she had ended up in the master bedroom at Porter Hall, she couldn't have him.

Eight

Sam paced back-and-forth across the library, her ponytail marking the time like a pendulum. Today was likely her last opportunity to locate any documents related to her grandparents if, and it was still an "if" in her mind, they had indeed worked for Chas' family. She'd been selfishly ignoring the possibility for days, afraid that if her past was rooted in this house, its history could stand between her and Chas.

She stopped to run a finger over the old ledgers that recorded the minutiae of the family's history. During last evening's phone call, Chas had made his intentions clear. He wanted her. Any reservations he may have had about having a personal relationship with an employee were obviously long gone. Sam had no doubt he would be back tonight to claim her as his. And she was longing for his strong arms around her, the slow beat of his heart through her skin. She closed her eyes remembering the weight and scent of him as they had lain by the stream. Every fiber of her being cried out for this man. But could she go to him with the past a dark cloud behind her?

Panic rose in her throat.

She'd known from the very beginning that the dance of anger, laughter and shared passion for their work was no mild flirtation. Their relationship was destined to be a serious one no matter how many times they stepped around their true feelings. What a conundrum. In the absence of her own parents, Grace and Patrick Quinn had given their granddaughter a loving home, a good education and the strength to weather any storm. Even after Sam's grandfather had died, Gran set aside her own pain to nurse her granddaughter's.

Tears clouded her vision. Part of Gran's strength had come from unwavering honesty; Sam knew to her very bones that truth had to be the basis of any future she might have with Chas. She owed her grandparents everything, yet even she had begun to doubt how such a valuable candlestick from a wealthy estate had made it across the Atlantic to take pride of place in a tiny clapboard house in Canada. It was time to put her fears behind her.

Whatever the answer proved to be, Sam could not, no, she would not, let anything besmirch her grandparents' memory. But first she needed to know for sure whether or not they had even worked at the Hall.

She scrubbed away her tears, and hoping against hope, began to rifle through the stack of ledgers on the library table. But she was wasting her time. These records were about wealth and possessions. Sam wracked her brain. She'd seen enough historical dramas to know those who lived "below stairs" never mixed with the family. Not even on paper.

What was it George had said? About the Burton-Porter grooms being Irish? It wasn't about where they were from, Sam realized with a start, it was about what they did. They were grooms! They lived and breathed horses, with even their living quarters over the stables. She should be looking in the tack room, not the library!

There was no time to waste.

Shoving the ledgers to one side, Sam tore through the house and across the courtyard to the stables. Max and Damien were grazing in the paddock, the Weekes had driven into town, and Chas was still in London. She had the place to herself.

Taking a deep breath, Sam slipped through the stable doors. Her nose twitched as soon as she was inside, instinctively telling her she was on the right path. She might forever associate the smell of roses with her Gran, but the comforting scent of leather and saddle soap was all Grampa. With a touch of liniment, she added, smiling to herself as she reached the tack room.

In Chas' grandfather's day, the Burton-Porters would have kept a string of thoroughbreds. Which required grooms, trainers and stable boys by the dozen. Not to mention equipment.

And this room, with its orderly collection of bridles, bits and stirrup leathers was at the heart of it all.

As Sam ran her fingers along the sculptured surface of a nearby saddle, thoughts of Chas and the way he'd kissed her here, in the tack room, threatened her resolve. "Go away Chas Porter," she whispered, "at least for now. I have to know who I am."

And once and for all unravel the mystery of the candlestick that had intrigued her since she was a small child.

Sam quickly scanned the room. Tucked away from the everyday business of riding, was an old oak bookcase, wedged in the far corner. Normally, a bookcase like that, with its three glass-covered shelves to keep the dust off its contents, would have been used in a law office, making it perfect for a busy stable. Fingers crossed that the case wasn't locked, Sam skirted the miscellaneous tack and disused feed pails for a closer look.

A puff of hay-scented dust rose in the air, as she rearranged the stacked boxes, making her sneeze and rub her hands over her face. How many years since any of this had been moved? After pushing aside a wooden box of odds and ends to reach the case, Sam spotted a trophy lying amid the tangle. Curious, she picked it up. It was tarnished and had a dent on its side. And an inscription: *Chas Porter, British Horse Society Junior Champion, Show Jumping, 1988*. It should be in pride of place, thought Sam, not tossed aside. She sighed for the little boy that was, and laid the trophy carefully back in the box.

Squatting down in front of the bookcase, Sam wiped the murky glass with her shirt tail and peered inside. The bookcase was full of ledgers! Hand shaking, she reached for the tiny brass knob and pulled the glass towards her. When it was level with the top of the shelf, she then slid it back, and like magic, it disappeared inside the cabinet. Quivering with anticipation, she plucked a brown leather ledger from the middle of the row and flicked it open. The spidery handwriting in fading brownish ink had to be over a hundred years old! Half the pages were blank, and the others were full of payments made to the local blacksmith and feed mill. The next six were the same. Sneezing, Sam quickly closed the lid and tried the next shelf down.

At least she was in the right century. The binding was less brittle and the ink less faded. These ledger entries were sporadic and written in several different hands, but the accounts were what she was after. Allowing for the swinging fortunes of the Burton-Porters and two world wars, it looked as though there was a high changeover in people as well as horses. Sam's pulse raced; she was getting closer.

Running her finger down the column, she saw more Irish surnames than not. George was right about that, she thought, as she passed Doyle and

O'Brien and Donnelly...and then Quinn, Patrick. Sam let out a muffled cry. Her grandfather! He'd been right here in this very room! Sam blinked back tears as she saw his weekly wages in the adjacent column. Even allowing for the passage of time, they were a pittance. Whoever had kept these records had had a system. If a man left during the year, a bold stroke was drawn through his name. Patrick Quinn's name had been crossed and re-crossed in the year he and Gran had emigrated to Canada.

Sam sat back on her heels. His name had been struck from the roster with vehemence. Sam's stomach clenched a little at the possibilities.

"Keep it calm," Sam told herself. "A fifty-year-old entry can't determine your life." Or could it?

In the distance, Sam heard a car door slam and then John Weekes called to the horses. Sam held her breath. She may have carte blanche around the house, but rooting through the records would be difficult to explain. Steadying herself, Sam set the open ledger on top of the bookcase and whipped out her mobile. With a swish of a finger, she was in camera mode, snapping a series of pictures. Then, after a last lingering look at her grandfather's name, Sam slipped the phone back inside her pocket and closed the ledger. At least, she thought, reluctantly putting the bookcase to rights, she would always have a record of his history.

As she threaded her way through the tack room, Sam could feel her earlier euphoria rapidly fading as she weighed the pros and cons of sharing what she'd discovered with Chas before she knew the whole story. Her grandfather had been employed here once, and he had left, possibly with some bad feelings based on his heavily crossed-out name in the ledger. Why would any of this matter to hers and Chas' relationship? Sam paused to let the scents of the stables and Porter Hall envelope her. It mattered because she loved Chas. She couldn't hide it from herself any longer. She had been taught to always face the truth, and this was a truth she had been so reluctant to acknowledge. Chas was her boss; he had his pick of eligible women; yet he had grown from a neglected boy to the warm and passionate man who set her pulse throbbing and her cheeks glowing just at the sound of his voice. He was domineering, autocratic, infuriatingly cool at times, but so kind and protective when he thought she had been hurt. He trusted her and sought her professional expertise for the emotional morass of cataloguing his inheritance.

She still felt a twinge of anger at the way he had blackmailed her into coming to his home, but there was gratitude as well. His actions had brought her to the source of her own shrouded heritage. Here she was, treading the same paving stones her grandfather had, breathing the same air, and even riding in the same meadows.

Pausing to grab a handful of carrots, Sam thought about her own journey as she walked, from a Toronto childhood filled with joy, to the hustle of the New York auction world and then on to the country her grandparents had left behind. It felt natural to be here, even if she was part interloper, possibly an outcome of Porter Hall's troubled past.

By the time she'd reached the courtyard, John Weekes was on the far side of the drive heading towards the back of the house, his arms laden with groceries.

Sam glanced towards the paddock.

Max and Damien were lazily nibbling at the grass, but at the sound of her approach, they were at the fence in a shot. "Okay, okay," she laughed holding a carrot in each hand. The carrots disappeared in a blur of twitching lips and chomping teeth. Sam repeated the process three times. Talk about unconditional love, she thought, as the two chestnuts nuzzled her in appreciation.

"Later," she cooed to Max. "We'll take a little ride, shall we?" She rubbed Damien's strong neck. "No sulking," she scolded, "you're too much for me to handle…besides you're already spoken for," she added squirming under the animal's baleful reproach. "Don't worry your big brown eyes, Damien. Chas will be home tonight."

As if on cue, the two chestnuts perked up their ears. Damien swung his massive head to where the gravel driveway wound its way up from the main road. A flash of metal through the trees caught Sam's attention and set her heart racing. A vehicle was coming up the drive. It was way too early for Chas to be coming home! She wasn't ready. She needed to absorb what she'd just learned and ride down to see George. Her forehead creasing, Sam peered into the distance. Then relaxed. The engine was wrong and just to prove it, a delivery van emerged from the shadows and continued towards the house.

"Who could that be?" she said aloud.

"That be the courier from Buxton," said a deep voice at her elbow. Sam yelped and spun around, hand over her heart, to see John Weekes. "Sorry, lass," he said, "didn't mean to startle you."

Sam gave out a nervous laugh. "I didn't hear you. I was too busy watching the van and spoiling these unruly beasts."

Damien tossed his head as if to say he deserved her attention.

But Sam swung back to the driveway, holding her hand over her eyes to shield it from the sun. John began to retrace his steps. "Are you expecting anything?" he asked over his shoulder.

"No," said Sam jogging to catch up. You?"

John shook his head as the van roared to a stop. The uniformed driver jumped out, clipboard in hand. "Afternoon," he called. He slid back the panel door and removed three large boxes, stacking one atop the other. "Miss Redfern?" he asked approaching Sam.

"Yes?"

He held out his clipboard. "Sign here, please."

Puzzled, Sam scanned the paperwork. The delivery was definitely for her. She scrawled her signature across the bottom and exchanged the clipboard for the boxes. "Here, let me," said John Weekes, holding out his arms.

Then his wife appeared and the three of them stood stock still watching the delivery truck zoom back down the driveway. "Oh, look," said Evelyn breaking the spell as she pointed to the label on the parcels. "They're from the saddlery near Buxton. Very posh, that is." She nodded for emphasis.

Sam blinked. Then gaped, then reached for the boxes. They were large, rectangular and identical in size. And suddenly, she knew what they were and who they were from. So must Evelyn, Sam thought as she looked up and saw the housekeeper's eyes shining with smug pleasure.

Flushing from the attention, Sam headed for the terrace, the Weekes following her like ducklings before Evelyn took charge and shooed her husband along, leaving Sam alone.

Heart thumping, Sam set the boxes on the garden table and slowly lifted the first lid. Inside, beneath the tissue paper was a beautiful pair of tall riding boots made of the most supple brown leather imaginable. She gasped with delight, and then eased the lids off the other two boxes. One held a pair of Wellington boots for mucking out the stalls, and the other contained leather paddock boots. Sam choked back a sob as she pulled them from their tissue and tried each one on in turn. She marveled at their elegance, prancing around the terrace like a modern-day Cinderella. How on earth had the man done it? Not only were the boots incredibly beautiful, they were a perfect fit.

Sam tugged her mobile from her pocket.

She called Chas' direct line, but no answer. He must have already left.

Which meant, depending on the traffic, he could be back at Porter Hall in less than four hours! Her body burned with longing at the thought of being in Chas' arms before the afternoon was out. And later, that evening…she glanced at her watch and almost freaked when she saw the time. Half the day was gone. Quickly, Sam gathered her new boots and repacked the boxes.

Thirty minutes later, she was astride Max flying across the meadow. Once Chas was home, it would be impossible for her to slip away to the home farm. And if George couldn't tell her what she needed to know, Sam wasn't sure what she'd do that evening.

She yearned for Chas more than she could say, but she wanted to meet him on equal footing without his childhood angst, her grandparents' hasty departure, or the whereabouts of the last candlestick hanging over their love like a black cloud.

The threads of the past had the power to either bind them together or tear them apart. She knew she had to tell him the truth. Otherwise, whatever was ahead of them in the future wouldn't be strong and true.

But what exactly was *he* hiding?

Obviously, debts had had to be paid; the Burton-Porters weren't the first family to sell off their heirlooms when estate taxes were introduced, and they wouldn't be the last. She'd seen more than enough evidence of that in the last few years.

But what was most peculiar, was that the candlestick collection had been dispersed piecemeal. If it had remained intact, it would have been worth a fortune. Obviously, Chas knew that, but why would the Burton-Porters have allowed it in the first place? Sam was more puzzled than ever.

Maybe after she spoke with George, she'd know what to do.

She saw his dog first. Robbie came racing across the farmyard, barking to announce their visit and intent on inspecting the newcomers, but a loud whistle from the house drew him up short. George appeared in the doorway of the farmhouse. Sam raised her arm and waved, as did he. It was a warm welcome. She quickly dismounted, gave Robbie her hand to sniff, and led Max through the gate, careful to secure it behind them.

"Afternoon." George greeted her, pulling out his hankie to wipe his hands as he walked towards her. "I was just making me tea. Will you have some?" His weathered eyes fixed on hers hopefully.

"Of course," said Sam. "It would be my pleasure. Besides," she added with a mischievous grin, "I have fresh scones." She reached into the saddlebag and pulled out her parcel, "Evelyn Weekes sent them for you."

"She looks after me, does Evelyn."

Leaving Max to nose about the yard with his reins dangling behind him, Sam followed George to the house, ducking her head as she crossed the threshold. It was like stepping back in time. The kitchen was snug and inviting, dominated by the cast-iron stove, the kettle on the boil, and the supper vegetables washed and ready. The stone floor had been swept so clean, it shone.

While George brewed the tea, Sam soaked up her surroundings. The farmhouse was really little more than a cottage, but every nook and cranny oozed history. The great divide from the Hall to this cozy hearth hadn't changed much, thought Sam. Her Gran would likely have grown up in a home like this. "George..." she began tentatively, "remember I told you my grandfather was Irish..."

"Aye." The old man plucked a plate from the shelf and began to arrange the scones on it. "A groom, weren't he?" He turned to face her.

"He was here," she blurted. "At Porter Hall." Her eyes searched his frantically, looking for confirmation that she hadn't dreamt it all.

George set the scones down on the table and drew out a chair opposite. He reached over and cupped Sam's hand in his. "When I said you had the look of the Irish about you, I had a particular fellow in mind."

"Really?" squeaked Sam.

"You're real natural like he was with the horses, and your hair's the right colour," smiled George, "temper, too, on occasion, I'd imagine."

"You knew my grandfather?"

"Aye…" said George, "…and your grandmother," he added softly.

A huge sob burst from the depths of Sam's very being. At long last, she'd found what she was looking for. She'd been rootless after her grandmother had died. And now here she was sitting in a cottage in Derbyshire across from someone who had known her grandparents when they were young. She mustn't be afraid of the past or she could lose her future with Chas. She must ask the questions that had plagued her these last few years, before the opportunity was lost.

Silently, George passed her a clean handkerchief, and waited while Sam blew her nose and wiped her wet cheeks. "What was she like?" Sam asked.

"She were lovely," George said, "kind and gentle, but feisty, too." A smile tugged at the corners of his mouth. "We were at school together until we were old enough to work. Your grandmother, she was a keen one. Found a place at a neighbouring estate. She were a housemaid at first…"

Sam nodded encouragingly. She mustn't let

think George think she was anything but proud of what her grandparents had accomplished, and where they had come from.

"There were a young lady there," George began, "took a shine to your grandmother from the beginning. Grace eventually became her maid. And went with her mistress when she married."

"That sounds like something out of a storybook..." faltered Sam.

George harrumphed. "Might have been if Chas' grandfather hadn't been the bridegroom."

"My grandmother was Eugenie Porter's maid!" Sam half-rose from her chair and then sat back down with a thump. She could hear the blood pounding in her ears. "But that means..."

George eyed her shrewdly. "That means," he repeated carefully, "that she had to be careful." He wasn't going to be any more specific, Sam knew. Chas' grandparents' marriage hadn't been a love match; it had been the continuation of the Burton-Porter brand.

"Your grandmother and Eugenie became fast friends in their own way," said George continuing his tale, "but even Eugenie couldn't help her when she got in the family way."

"My grandmother was..." she breathed.

"Aye," said George. "When Chas' grandfather found out, there were a terrible row. Paddy had poached on 'his rights' by taking up with Grace. The arrogant fool was all set to horsewhip your grandfather, but Paddy weren't having none of it. He stood up for himself. Knocked Chas' grandfather out cold."

Sam's heart was pounding wildly. "Does Chas know?" she asked.

"Maybe he does, and maybe he don't."

"And my grandmother?" Sam asked in a shaky breath.

"It was Eugenie, Chas' grandmother, who sorted it. Bundled Grace up before the old man came to," his eyes narrowed, "That candlestick you're itching to ask me about, that were a wedding gift. Eugenie swore Grace not to ever say where she got it, but it weren't stolen, if that's what you been thinking."

"How do you know all this?"

"My mother worked at the Hall. She were there the night it happened. The old man shut himself in the study with a bottle of whiskey and it were all hushed up."

"And the other candlesticks?" Sam prodded. "What about them?"

The old man's jaw clenched. "Let the young lad tell you himself. I don't want nowt to do with it." They sat in silence for a moment. George's eyes misted over. "Grace was a beautiful woman. I was sorry to see her go…even though I liked Paddy, well enough."

"They were happy," Sam said gently, giving his calloused hand a squeeze. "I wish she'd been able to tell me about her life here." "Don't be letting the old days get in the way for you. And don't be fooled into thinking Chas will either. I didn't think I was good enough for your grandmother once she went up to the Hall. And I lost her." The old man cleared his throat. "Be nice to have you around the place."

"I think I'm going to cry again," whispered Sam.

"I best get the tea then," said George. He got to his feet and lumbered across the room, returning a moment later with two cups of well-milked tea. "It'll all work out, lass, you'll see."

When tea was over, Sam planted a kiss on George's cheek and slipped out the door. George waved her on her way. "Time to get a move on," he told her with an experienced look at the sky. "It's coming on to rain."

Sam returned his goodbye and gathered up Max's reins. Her head and her emotions churned with the history George had unfolded. And the weather was reflecting her mood, she realized. Above, the clouds raced across the sky as the blue of the afternoon became shrouded with the coming storm. Max danced a little under her and then set off at a willing trot, eager to be back in his stable.

Hoping she could make it back before the rain fell, Sam urged him to a full gallop, cresting the hill just as Chas' car sped toward the Hall.

The afternoon light was rippling through the leaves as Chas guided the sleek vehicle up the lane leading to the Hall. What a difference a week had made in his life! He was coming home with a grin on his face, an unheard of occurrence. Over the years, he'd found so many excuses to avoid Porter Hall, he'd almost forgotten how much the estate meant to him. It had taken Sam, reluctant at first, and then full of warmth and passion, to show him what was really important in life.

Perhaps it was time to send Chas "bloody" Porter packing.

They could spend their weekdays in London and then motor down at the weekend. It would take nothing more than a phone call to have Max and Damien brought over on a regular basis and, with Sam around, the house would feel alive again.

He didn't need to check his reflection to know he was grinning from ear-to-ear as he pictured Sam waiting for him. He pressed harder on the accelerator. His heart had been stone cold for so long, he'd forgotten the rush of warmth a home could bring.

This was the way it should be.

As he rounded the last curve, a finger of sunlight escaped the gathering clouds and illuminated the figures of Sam and Max flying over the hill. With the distant sheets of coming rain obscuring the meadows behind them, wisps of her brilliant hair sparked in the stray light like flares from the sun. Max's glossy flanks shone giving the whole scene a look of a warrior maiden from myth riding hell-bent to greet her lover.

Chas groaned softly, his pleasure at homecoming yielding to his overmastering desire. It would be all he could do to be civil before taking Sam on a personal tour of his bedroom.

He slowed the car and lowered the window, waiting for her to trot toward him. With immense satisfaction he noted that she was wearing the boots he had sent for her. For a moment he imagined her wearing only the boots. With effort, he banished the enticing picture from his mind.

Max pranced a little beside the car as Sam reined him in. She laughed and patted his neck. "Steady, sweetheart. Let's just take a moment to be polite," she crooned to him and turned her smiling face toward Chas. "The rain is making him nervous."

"The weatherman is predicting quite a storm," Chas returned. He cursed himself silently for the inanity of his response, but when his heart was pounding so, it was hard to be witty.

"Guess I'd better get him back to the stable, then," said Sam turning Max's head.

"See you at the house."

"Nice paint job by the way!" Sam yelled over her shoulder.

With a deep chuckle, Chas waited until they had gone a safe distance and then raced the car the rest of the way up the drive. Not bothering to unload his bag, he hurried back to the stable. Sam had already unsaddled Max and led him into his stall. She had just started grooming the horse when Chas came up behind her. She turned her head but instead of speaking, Chas leaned into her, cradling her body with his. His strong hands covered her small ones as she reached to smooth the brushes across Max's neck.

Sam stilled a moment, and then continued to groom the horse, his hands on hers, his arms enclosing her own. Their breaths, at first ragged, eased and melded into one rhythm. The warmth of their embrace slipped through their clothing so that her skin was warmed by his, and he by her. He laid his rough cheek against her smooth one; her hair curled against his neck and caressed him.

The reality of such a joyous homecoming was so strong, Chas could hardly breathe.

When Max was sufficiently groomed, Sam turned in his arms and her eyes, luminous and starry bright looked up into his. He leaned into the kiss they had both been waiting for, his lips at first soft and tender, brushing her cheek, her jawline, and then smoothing softly across her own. Their ardor surged; his kisses became harder, more demanding. She pressed against him, clearly longing to take in as much as he would offer. The fever of that possessive, thrusting kiss lasted eons, ricocheting through their entire beings, channeling all of his passion toward this one precious woman.

The kiss might have lasted for hours, but for Max, butting Chas impatiently. The horse knew he had given good service and was entitled to his ration of oats.

Sam and Chas broke apart laughing. Sam lowered her eyes and retrieved the grooming combs, while Chas fetched the oats. Without speaking they tidied the stable, ensured the horses had all they needed and then, hand-in-hand left the stable.

Raindrops were starting to fall and the wind had picked up as Chas got his belongings from the boot of the car. Sam finger-combed her hair and shyly pulled a wisp of straw from her sweater. Noting the signs of feminine preening, Chas felt yet another swell of joy.

Gripping her hand again, they mounted the stone steps and entered the house.

If ever there was a symbol that times had changed, Sam thought, it was this entrance with Chas. Her grandmother, even as the close friend of the lady of the house would have entered by the kitchen door. Her grandfather had probably never set foot in the house at all.

The Weekes were nowhere to be seen. A note on the dining room table indicated that the housekeeper had retired with a headache and had left a tray for them in the kitchen.

Chas raised his eyebrows. "I don't remember Mrs. Weekes ever having a headache," he said, a slight smile tugging the corner of his lips. His amazingly wonderful lips, Sam thought. "I suspect she is being discreet."

They grinned at each other like children. Chas leaned close to whisper conspiratorially, "I'm not sure I fully explained all the treasures that are in my bedroom. Shall we give them a look over now that I'm here?"

"It wouldn't be professional not to," Sam agreed.

Together, they ran up the stairs, the old house echoing with their laughter. When they entered his bedchamber, and Chas gently closed the door behind them, all desire to laugh left Sam. Instead, she overflowed with a slow joy as she turned to face the man she loved. She opened her arms and he stepped forward to claim her. Once again his head bent to hers in a slow, masterful kiss. She returned it with searing passion. Her arms rose to his shoulders, then around his neck, fingers playing with his soft hair. He in turn, stroked her back and, while the kisses went on, gently, he spun her toward the waiting bed. He paused. Smiling, she took his hand and led him the rest of the way.

Outside the storm broke. While rain and wind lashed against the windows, sheets of lightning flashed across the landscape. The power of the storm mirrored the ecstasy they unleashed in each other's arms. Thunder echoed to Sam's cries of pleasure and the wind chorused Chas' groans of passion satisfied.

Afterwards, as they lay listening to the rumbling thunder and tapping rain, Sam knew she had never been so happy. With a faint start of guilt she realized that in her joy at having Chas home again, in accepting the love he offered her, she had not spoken about her own connection to this house. And she had to do that. She had to face her past as it would be reflected in her lover's eyes. Or else there would be no future for them.

Her thoughts were interrupted by a soft kiss from Chas. "You're frowning."

Sam summoned a smile. Now was not the time. "Just realizing I'm a bit hungry."

"Miss Redfern, do you mean you want more?" he teased.

"Are you offering?"

"For you, always." He caught her in his arms again and for quite a while her mind completely forgot her stomach.

Later, completely warm and satisfied, she sighed. He pulled himself up beside her and kissed the tip of her nose. "I think it's time to raid the kitchen and see what Mrs. Weekes has left for us."

Wrapped in robes, they made their way down to the kitchen, just as the lights flickered and went out, leaving them in total darkness. Sam squeaked and clutched Chas' arm. Then, stumbling and laughing, they felt their way to a cupboard housing emergency candles.

Mission accomplished, they sat in the window seat of Chas room, Sam in his lap as they watched the storm slowly retreat from the fields. They ate their fill of the delicacies provided by Mrs. Weekes, and finished their evening with a superb wine.

Sam leaned against Chas' chest, feeling his heartbeat mirroring her own. She had never felt so completely and utterly happy. But tomorrow she would have to tell him the truth. She took another sip of wine and kissed his neck. Tomorrow.

Nine

The gray dawn crept across the bedroom highlighting Chas' strong features, relaxed now in sleep. Sam gazed at him tenderly, the warmth of her love and the heat from their first night together washing over her as the sun rose above the horizon.

Their lovemaking had filled Sam in a way she had not thought possible. By turns passionate and gentle, abandoned and considerate, she had never imagined that love could be like this. Chas' eyes opened and a smile of love and longing suffused his expression. He reached for her again…

Later, when Sam cut through the kitchen to say a quick good morning to Evelyn Weekes, she found herself blushing like a schoolgirl. "Breakfast will be ready in a tick," she heard Evelyn call after her.

Sam could sense the delight in the housekeeper's voice. It was no match for her own joy, but it warmed Sam's heart to know they had her approval.

Outside, the day was uncharacteristically gloomy.

But with Chas waiting for her on the terrace, not even the threat of another rain storm could dampen Sam's spirits or dim the afterglow from a night spent in her boss's arms. Not to mention the morning...

"I love your smile," said Chas, his eyes sleepily raking her over as she approached the table. "Thinking about anything in particular?" he asked.

"Could be." She sat down across from him, teasing with her comments and leaning towards him in a seductive pose. She could hardly believe this brazen behaviour of hers. It had roared to the surface with each kiss and every embrace. Chas had made her feel confident and strong. Any doubts she had about whether or not he would find her sexy had vanished beneath the heat of his passion.

She was free to flirt. "And you?" she teased. "Anything on your mind?"

"Breakfast?"

"You are so male!"

"I didn't hear any complaints earlier." He was enjoying himself way too much, Sam decided. She was all set to snuggle onto his lap and remind him again just how male he was, when Evelyn stepped onto the terrace staggering beneath the weight of a heavily-loaded tray.

Chas jumped to his feet and went to his housekeeper's aid, whispering something in her ear that Sam couldn't hear. Smiling brightly, Sam concentrated on not showing her embarrassment as Chas helped Evelyn arrange a full breakfast with juice and coffee and all the trappings. Thank goodness, there wasn't a full complement of staff to confront.

Sleeping with the lord of the manor had its downside even with the apparent approval of the residents of the house. Inevitably, her thoughts drifted back to her grandmother, a young servant girl with child, living and working in an unhappy household while her future husband toiled in the stables. There would have been no smiles of approval for her.

She must have been so frightened. And then, so brave.

Swallowing back the threat of tears, Sam resolved that tonight before she slipped, hopefully, into Chas' arms once again, she would tell him everything. About their grandmothers, about the friendship between them, and the disastrous night the young couple had fled Porter Hall carrying a silver candlestick given to them by Eugenie Burton-Porter, insurance against an unknown future.

"Sam?"

The smell of freshly roasted coffee and crispy bacon cut through her thoughts. She was famished.

"Thank you, Evelyn!" Sam called to the housekeeper's retreating back. "Mmm," she cooed as she took her first bite. "I could get used to this."

"We're getting the special treatment, in case you hadn't noticed…"

"Actually, I had from the moment we arrived. But then…" Sam reached for her coffee, "you are the apple of your housekeeper's eye."

"And yours?"

His eyes bored into hers, bluer than she'd ever seen them. And her body tingled with anticipation. He was demanding an answer, but what to say? Until they cleared the air, any conversation about the future lay on shaky ground. Not only was she frightened of how he would react to her news about their family connection, she had to continually remind herself that Chas was her boss. Porter Hall had buffered them from the reality of London, but in two days, they would be back in the office trying to pick up a normal rhythm. A normal rhythm which would be microscopically examined by everyone at Burton-Porter.

Sam shivered. So much depended on her answer.

Across the table, Chas watched and waited while Sam struggled with what he'd meant as a light-hearted response to her joust.

A feeling of unease surged through him. Was she having second thoughts, or simply adjusting to the new reality of their situation? Whatever it was, he had to tread carefully. She had become so precious to him, so integral to his happiness, that he could not bear to lose her. But where their relationship was going, he was still not sure.

There was their work and positions at Burton-Porter to consider, although he felt confident that they would fall into the normal pattern between boss and employee once they were in the office. Sam was smart enough to protect his privacy, and her own, of course.

Lord, he sounded like a prat! This was no illicit affair. He need look no further than the achingly beautiful woman opposite him to know that this was the real deal. But her averted eyes and the napkin being pleated between her fingers showed her sudden anxiety. If he was true to his feelings, he should immediately reassure her that their love-making had been driven by more than lust.

"Hey! It was just a bit of playful banter…which you started as I recall." He relaxed into a smile.

"Sorry," said Sam. "It's not every day a girl wakes up to find she's living a dream." The shadow which flitted across her face didn't match her words.

Something was definitely troubling Miss Samantha Redfern, and Chas was damn sure he knew what it was. Those bloody candlesticks again.

He got abruptly to his feet. Keeping his voice as light and carefree as possible, he suggested they go for a ride to clear the cobwebs. "And then," he announced, "we really must tackle those last files in the library."

He could tell by the way Sam hurriedly began to gather their breakfast dishes that his flash of anger hadn't gone unnoticed. "Just leave them," he ordered. "Mrs. Weekes can see to them." He strode off knowing he was acting like a fool, but his pride was hurt, and what had seemed so easy last night was suddenly fraught with complications.

Was it any wonder he'd avoided building a serious relationship with anyone before? If this was love, than maybe it wasn't for him. It certainly wasn't part of his history. Bleakly, he wondered if he was doomed by his family's past, or if he could break free from their miserable traditions of hard arrogance and greed.

And then a hand grabbed his arm and tugged until he broke his stride. He spun around, all fire and ice, took one look at Sam's crumpled face and folded her into his arms.

"You really are the apple of my eye," she sobbed into his chest. "I just...got a little overwhelmed, that's all..." As she tipped her head back, the sun broke through the clouds. Her tears turned into emeralds and he knew he was lost.

"I love you, Samantha Redfern."

Sam sat at the library table, pleasantly tired from the brisk ride across the fields, hands threaded through her hair as she mulled over what was now a nagging question.

How on earth could she tell Chas about her connection to the Hall without breaking the magic? On the backs of the horses and then during their care in the stable, there had not been any opening to broach the subject. Face it, Sam, she told herself, every moment had been so perfect she had been afraid to shatter them with an ill-timed revelation. And so she had retreated immediately to the library, with the only declaration being that she had a few last files to sort.

Blissfully, she wandered to the window and reveled in the beauty of the rolling countryside. Her heart thumped and an idiotic grin spread across her face. He'd told her he loved her!

Without any doubt, she knew that she loved him, and she truly believed he'd meant his own declaration to her. But love had to be unconditional if it was going to work, and obviously, they didn't trust each other. At least, not completely.

Methodically, Sam began to tick off the obstacles in their path. She had made it clear to Chas from the beginning that her background was very different from his, in itself not so bad. But unbeknownst to both of them, her grandparents had worked for his and the last candlestick bound them together in the most unusual way.

With Sam claiming her interest in the eleventh candlestick was a professional one, and Chas not showing her his collection, it was the pot calling the kettle black. And yet when she'd discovered his set, they'd had a terrible row. He still didn't know about the other candlestick back in her flat, and now she was too scared to tell him.

She had no excuse. Not now, not after what George had told her about their shared family history. The rest of the story had to come from Chas, he'd told her. Let him explain.

But he hadn't.

And nor had she.

But she was going to as soon as she finished packing up those last catalogue notes.

She was, in fact, lowering the lid on the box when Chas returned a half-hour later. "Nice timing." Her heart leapt at the way the air charged as the room filled with his presence.

When he didn't respond, she glanced up to see him striding towards her, muscles rippling with masculine intent. Still clad in jeans and t-shirt from their earlier ride, he was a magnificent sight. Sam felt her mouth go dry.

She edged away from the table, her earlier determination completely forgotten.

He was upon her now, so close the heat from their bodies met and mingled in a cloud of musky desire.

"If you have any complaints about my work ethic, Miss Redfern…" Chas breathed in her ear, "feel free to take them up with management. In fact…" he nipped the tip of her lobe, "why not take them directly to your boss…but do be careful, he can be very demanding."

With that, he cupped her bottom and drew her closer and closer until she could feel just how demanding he could be.

He backed up against the library table and slid his hands down the backs of her thighs, parting her legs and lifting her until she found herself straddling him, her knees resting on the table top.

Erotic images crowded her vision. Her breath quickened to light, fast inhalations of his male scent. Forgetting her resolve and the setting, she reached for him.

"Would you like me to set up drinks on the terrace?" Mrs. Weekes called from the depths of the hallway.

Blushing wildly, Sam broke away; Chas grinned wickedly. "Not tonight, Mrs. Weekes, but thank you," he replied, not a tremor in his voice.

He twirled a loose strand of Sam's hair around his fingers. "Mmm," he inhaled. "We have time for a stroll down to the stables before dinner."

Sam batted his hand away. "Oh, no you don't, not until I've had time to shower and change. And…and I am quite hungry." She caught his expression and hastily added. "For dinner, I mean."

Chas smiled and lowered his head to hers. "I'm guessing you have more than one little black dress with you," he breathed.

Uncertain, Sam nodded.

"So how would you feel about wearing one to dinner this evening? It is, after all, our last night together."

Sam cleared her throat. "Chas…there's something I need to tell you…"

"All you ever need to tell me is how much you love me…" He looked down at her, his blue eyes piercing her to her soul. "In fact I've been waiting all day to hear you tell me."

"I…I love you beyond measure," she blurted. "But, I must…"

He cut her off with a long, deep kiss. "No, we must celebrate…we have an hour until dinner," he whispered huskily.

Sam wriggled away from him, heart pounding, feeling a little too breathless for comfort. "Then I had better get moving. It wouldn't be professional to keep my boss waiting."

She nearly ran from the library, equally intent on escaping the throbbing passion Chas raised in her as in making herself as desirable as possible for the man she loved. Later perhaps, the timing would be better for her revelations. Besides, she told herself, if this was going to be their last evening together at Porter Hall, it wouldn't hurt for him to be fully aware of what he had to lose.

Even in her quick movements as she scurried down the corridor and entered her room, she realized how much she had come to love this entire house. The setting sun slanted through her window and the slight breeze that flitted through the open casement carried the fresh scent of thriving vegetation and the soothing symphony of the English countryside – bawling sheep, a horse's whinny and the distant rumble of a motor.

Sam paused to breathe deeply. In less than a week, all of this had come to symbolize the hidden side of Chas, the soul of the man hidden behind the cool surface of the sophisticated businessman. And knowing both sides of him, she loved him all the more.

Purposefully, Sam cast aside her working clothes and stepped into the hot shower, lingering a little as the water streamed like her lover's touch over her soaped body. The finest gold-fitted shower at the

New York Plaza Hotel could not have given her the pleasure that this one gave. Because no matter how sophisticated or fun the evening waiting for her turned out to be, no evening would ever feel right again unless Chas was waiting for her.

She dried herself and stood naked in front of the mirror. She was delighted with her body because Chas had been delighted. All the imperfections she had once fussed over melted from her awareness. She knew she was beautiful.

Her lingerie was new and lacy, purchased to fit perfectly under the dress she had intended for the Sotheby's cocktail party. The dress flowed across her skin, silky and flattering. Her chosen jewelry, small emerald stones in her ears to emphasize her green eyes, and a simple matching necklace that drew the eyes discreetly to her cleavage. She loved the soft feel of the brush stroking through her hair before she swept it up and the cool scent of her carefully applied makeup. She considered a spritz of perfume but decided instead to leave the soap's lingering scent of roses on her skin.

She stood a moment in the middle of the room, savoring the silence and the sense of herself perfectly suited to this place. No matter what her origins, it was time for her to come home. Unconsciously, her eyes drifted to the candlestick. A less-than-gentle reminder of how easily she had set aside her earlier determination to tell Chas everything. She had let the moment pass, and slid into his arms instead.

Distantly, she heard the clock strike and giving herself a little shake, Sam threw off the weight of the past for the desires of the future. She left her room and walked confidently down the corridor, pleased with the swish of fabric around her thighs. Reaching the main staircase, she paused. Chas waited at the bottom, eyes lighting at the sight of her. He wore a tux, the crisp, white shirt highlighting his tanned face, and the fitted jacket emphasizing the broad width of his shoulders, powerful chest, and lean hips.

Sam's heart beat a little faster.

Chas looked up and saw the woman of his dreams pause at the head of the stairs. Her hand rested lightly on the banister as she slowly descended toward him. For an instant, he had a vision of his ancestors descending like Sam, resplendent in the fashions of their time, elegant, sure of themselves. His heart swelled. They had had every advantage, wealth, poise and position, but he doubted that any had been as beloved as this beauty before him.

He reached out, took her hand and raised it; his lips brushed gently against the backs of her fingers, his gesture of honor and respect for this amazing woman.

Yet even as he drank in Sam's undeniable loveliness, Chas knew that if honor was as important to him as he claimed, he had to share all of his past with her.

As he led her into the dining room, her quick intake of breath filled him with pride, and with trepidation. Evelyn Weekes had outdone herself. The room was aglow with the light of ten candles. It was probably the first time in more than fifty years that the collection had been on display. He felt Sam's fingers tighten on his arm. "They're spectacular," she whispered. "It's like walking into a dream."

Wordlessly, Chas reached over and covered her hand with his. They noted the chaffing dishes waiting for them on the sideboard, the pair of candles standing elegantly upright in the silver candlesticks at either end, and then turned to take in the gleaming mahogany table. Mrs. Weekes had prepared the place settings so that they could sit across from each other flanked by the remaining candlesticks. It was exactly as Chas had requested. The candlesticks had been grouped in two sets of three to create an oasis of intimacy in the middle of the table. The candle flames flickered ever so slightly as Chas escorted Sam to her seat. "Miss Redfern," he said releasing her so that he could pull out her chair.

She reached up to stroke his cheek. "Mr. Porter," she replied.

And then with innate grace, she turned, smoothing her dress beneath her as she sat, as elegant and serene as her surroundings. She wore her hair up, and Chas lingered a moment, mentally ravishing his beloved as he trailed his fingers down the nape of her neck, reveling in the softness of her skin and the delicate scent of her hair.

Breaking the spell, he shifted gears and moved to the end of the table where a bottle of sparkling wine lay waiting in an elaborate silver bucket. His eyes met hers in invitation.

"Please," was all he needed to hear. Chas plucked the bottle from its resting place, wrapped it in a white napkin and popped the cork with a flourish. Sam laughed delightedly, and the evening began in earnest. Seared scallops with ginger and lime, beef bourguignon, and a lemon sorbet followed by a chocolate torte and coffee.

His housekeeper, had indeed, outdone herself.

"What shall we drink to now?" said Chas returning from the sideboard with a small glass of cognac for each of them.

"Hmm," said Sam, touching the glass to her lips. "We've toasted us. Mrs. Weekes…"

"Many times," Chas agreed.

"Burton-Porter…Great-Aunt Agnes…Max and Damien…" her eyes danced in the candlelight. "Remember the first time we ate together. At that chichi restaurant in…wherever…"

God, she was gorgeous, Chas grinned. It had been quite a meal and he'd savored every minute of it. In fact, they both had, laughing over their initial bickering, the fall in the mud and all the daily adventures and misadventures as they grew closer and closer. "The restaurant was in the Cotswolds."

"Right." Sam nodded. "And you said, 'is there anything we might drink to without getting into a fight?'"

"And then you said, 'how about my impeccable taste in silver'?" And there it was, the subject they'd both been avoiding all night. Chas watched the light fade from Sam's eyes as she realized the import of her words. She set her glass to one side.

"It's time, isn't it?" she said, her hand reaching across the table for his, just as he'd reached for hers in the restaurant. Her touch had electrified him then, and it still did, but now it was filled with love and longing…and hope.

"Before we go any further, I have something to tell you," said Chas, "about the candlesticks. I was never just collecting them, I was buying them back, as my grandmother had done, in an effort to restore the family name." He could feel his jaw tighten as he spoke, telling Sam how his grandfather had dishonored his wife and their home by his lecherous ways. "Before they were married, he had had free rein, claiming more than one young woman from the estate who feared for her livelihood and that of her family, if she dared refuse his advances. When things became…. awkward, he paid them off."

His eyes were like glaciers. The distaste he felt for the havoc his grandfather had wreaked upon those who depended upon him and upon the estate for their very existence, had dogged him all his life. "And just to make matters worse," he continued, "he bought them off, not with money, but with plate, giving them exquisite candlesticks that they were unable to sell for fear of being accused of stealing." Chas could feel his throat constrict. He released Sam's hand to reach for his cognac, but as he raised it to his mouth, he saw that her face was as white as the linen.

"Is this too much?"

Sam shook her head. "No, no. Please, go on." She clenched her hands under the table where he couldn't see them. His confession petrified her, yet filled her with resolve at the same time. He was fighting one of his biggest demons by sharing his deepest fears with her. She could do no less now that she knew the truth about her own family.

Chas sighed. "My poor grandmother had no idea. She was the sacrificial lamb, you see, young, beautiful and wealthy. Her father arranged everything with his daughter's future husband. I'm sure in the earlier months, my grandmother thought theirs was what a marriage should be, and then my father was born. Once he had his heir, my grandfather simply picked up where he had left off, leaving my grandmother to cope, or not, as she saw fit." Chas snorted, and took another drink.

The candles had burned down over the evening; their light cast harsh shadows across the rigid panes of her lover's face. Sam's heart went out to him.

"How many?" She heard herself whisper.

"Candlesticks? Only two were left when he died, seven when I inherited. My father couldn't have cared less about the collection, but my grandmother did. She scoured the valley, quietly buying back the five she found. Making amends the best she could."

"And the rest?" Sam asked, hoping he hadn't noticed the quiver in her voice.

"I used my connections; let certain dealers know I was interested." Chas waved his arm to encompass the candlesticks positioned about the room. "It took me years to find the next three. And then there you were, bidding on number eleven." His fingers curled around his glass. "Luckiest day of my life! I know I should have told you sooner, Sam, but it's not an easy story to share. With anyone. Even you. I was afraid of what you would think of my family, and of me." His jaw twitched. "Forced to outbid the boss, and then blackmailed into accompanying him to Porter Hall. For a while, even I thought I was just following family tradition, taking advantage of the power they held over those who worked for them. But you understood and you trusted me when not many others would."

Sam swallowed hard. The irony was not lost on her as she prepared to test Chas' mettle even further. "Do you have any idea..." she asked, "where the twelfth candlestick is?"

"Yes, and no. But I don't think we'll ever get our hands on it."

"Why not?"

Chas' eyes glinted like steel daggers. "Because according to my father, it disappeared along with my grandmother's maid and one of the grooms. My father was a boy at the time, but he remembered the gossip. There had been a fight. Over the maid. And my grandfather swore if he ever saw either of them again, he'd have them both horsewhipped and thrown in jail."

Sam couldn't hold back a gasp. This was getting more complicated by the minute. "What about your grandmother? What did she say?"

Chas shook his head. "She had already passed away by the time my father told me the story. Not that it would have made any difference. The candlestick is likely beyond reach. They probably went to Australia…or maybe even Canada."

"It was Canada," whispered Sam.

The room went still. Across the table, Chas literally froze in place. She could see his mind racing to make sense of what she had just said. For the first time, another horrible fear occurred to her, that he might think she set the whole thing up from the time she arrived in England and went to work for Burton-Porter. But she hadn't known, not really, where to start or what to look for. It had been about finding out who she was and where the candlestick fit into her family history. She had her answers, and now Chas deserved to hear them before he jumped to any more wrong conclusions.

"Your grandmother and mine were more than mistress and servant," she started tentatively,

"They were friends. My grandmother's name was Grace, by the way. She was lovely and hard-working and honest as the day is long. She was your grandmother's maid before she was married and came with her to Porter Hall."

"It fits perfectly with everything you've just told me," she went on. "But your father had it wrong. My grandmother was in love with a groom, Patrick Quinn. They wanted to get married, but had to keep their plans secret until they had enough money. Unfortunately, my grandmother became pregnant. She couldn't hide it forever. And once your grandfather caught wind of it, he was furious. You know he considered the household staff his property. He went down to the stables with his horsewhip, only my grandfather knocked him out cold before he had a chance to use it. It was your grandmother who gave them the candlestick and sent them on their way."

Exhaustion swept over Sam as she waited for Chas' response.

It came with an ice-cold fury. "I don't know what you're playing at, Samantha Redfern, but my grandmother spent the rest of her life trying to undo the damage her husband, and then her son, caused this family. And not once did she make any mention of your grandmother."

But Sam was not backing down. "I grew up with that candlestick," she said. "In a tiny home in Toronto. With very little money, but with kindness and honour and love. I only knew two things about that candlestick. That it was precious and that there were more like it back in England; any more than that my grandmother would not say." Sam's heart was pounding so loudly, she could barely think. Even she had had doubts about her grandparents once she realized the connection. But not anymore. As much as she loved Chas, she had to set the record straight, even if it meant losing him.

"Unlike the others," she began, "my grandparents could have easily sold the candlestick. Lots of people emigrated with something portable that they could sell or barter to help them get a new start. But my grandparents never would…your grandmother had made mine promise to never tell anyone how they came by the candlestick, she was that afraid of her husband. So my grandmother never did."

Chas leapt to his feet. "I don't believe this!" He began to pace back and forth, his anger driving him on. Sam's head throbbed as she fought to remain strong. It wouldn't have mattered when she told him; it was easier for him to believe what he'd been told years earlier, than accept that his beloved grandmother had given away a candlestick even if it had been because of her husband's behaviour.

Chas whirled around and came back to stand opposite. "So where's the candlestick now?" he demanded.

Sam's chin went up. "In my flat."

Gripping the back of his chair, Chas glared at her across the table. "How could you not tell me this before?"

"Because I didn't know the whole story until yesterday. And while we're on the subject, what's your excuse?"

"I don't need one."

Sam was on her feet now, stunned by the dire turn of events.

"It was George, wasn't it? That's why you went to see him!" Chas' voice stung with accusation.

Eyes blazing, Sam nodded curtly. "I found a reference to my grandfather in the tack room. He had worked here as a groom. And then all the pieces fell into place, except one...George had known my mother when she was young. And his mother was assisting in the kitchens that evening at the Hall. She helped your grandmother cover her tracks."

"Seeing as you can't bring yourself to believe me, you can verify my story with George, Mr. Porter." She tossed her napkin on the table. "I think it's time we said 'good night.'"

"Fine with me," snapped Chas.

"In fact," said Sam, "I'll find my own way back to London."

"I'll have John run you to the station in the morning."

"Do that," retorted Sam. Head held high, she walked around the table and out the door, her knees wobbling so hard, she had no idea how she remained upright. As she mounted the stairs of Porter Hall to gather her things, she felt her heart shatter into a million pieces.

Glass slippers were for fairy tales.

Alone in the dining room, Chas felt as though every drop of blood had drained from his body. He'd gambled on gaining Sam's trust by telling her how vile his grandfather had been and how shamefully the Burton-Porter men had treated their women. And what had he received in the end? Nothing but a massive betrayal. Samantha Redfern, the woman he'd come to love with all his heart, had known about the candlesticks from the start.

Or had she?

He refilled his glass and sat down, but as he raised the cognac to his lips, all he could see was the burnished copper of his sweetheart's hair shinning in the candlelight. A groan escaped him. He loved her. He knew she loved him, yet this incredible wedge had just come between them, splitting them apart at the very moment they should be planning a future together.

The remains of their romantic dinner were all around him, mocking him for his stupidity.

And there was no one to blame but himself. He was the one who'd brought her to Porter Hall in the first place. He knew in his heart that her surprise at the auction had been genuine, just as her chagrin at being coerced into helping him catalogue the estate had been the real thing.

He toyed with the idea of rousting George out of bed, but that would be ludicrous. It was late, George was an old man, and if there was one thing he knew about Samantha Redfern, she did not lie. Like him, she might omit a few facts now and then, but he couldn't fault her honesty. In fact, he thought sitting up straighter, had she wanted to, she could have kept the whole story about the candlestick to herself. He would never have been the wiser.

Was it true then?

Had her grandmother and his been close enough to conspire against his grandfather? He quickly reviewed what he'd told Sam, and realized that when he combined his knowledge with hers, it had the ring of truth about it.

He needed to think, and think hard. Putting aside his cognac and grabbing a candlestick from the table, Chas went around the room carefully snuffing out the remaining candles. Then, he navigated his way to the gallery by candlelight.

Strolling its length with a heavy heart reminded him that the relatives and the history he'd lived with all his life, was a burden he no longer wished to bear. That was why he had planned to sell Porter Hall. But then Sam had entered his house and his life and it seemed that the dark history had lightened, been banished by their growing love. It didn't matter that he and Sam had been reluctant to take that final leap of faith; the importance lay in that they had offered their secrets to each other. And then he'd shut her down.

He'd been wrong. He had thought he could mend the past by reclaiming its squandered treasures. Now he knew that the past must be healed by his honour and a love built on unquestioning trust.

He would not grill George for confirmation of Sam's story. He would believe it because she believed it, and she had offered it to him – a heritage as dear to her as any this old house could harbour. He groaned. Were there any more tests of fire needed to burn away the weight of his inheritance?

Heart pounding, he moved through the silent house with new-found purpose. He would tell Sam how much he loved her, that he believed her, and that whatever had happened in the past, was just that. Ancient history.

But when he reached her door, he hesitated. He'd wounded her so badly, he wouldn't blame her if she never spoke to him again. But he had to try. Raising his hand, he knocked softly. There was no response. He pressed his forehead against the door and waited. Still nothing. Silently cupping his hand around the doorknob, he gave it a slight turn, hoping he could at least whisper her name or even hear her gently breathing. But it was locked.

He wanted to pound on her door and demand her forgiveness, but that would only prove that he had been right all along. That he was just another in a long line of arrogant Burton-Porter males, and he didn't deserve her.

That perhaps it was already too late.

Ten

Fumbling with exhaustion, Sam unlocked the door to her flat, braced it with her shoulder, and tugged her cases over the threshold, scattering the dust motes that had collected in her absence. With a sigh of relief, she allowed the door to shut firmly behind her.

It had been a miserable journey back to London. Slipping down the back stairs while it was still dark had made her feel like a thief in the night. But she'd managed to avoid seeing Chas, and after the abrupt end to their last evening together at Porter Hall, Sam was thankful for small mercies.

Desperate to run from the pain, she'd waited in the shadows by the coach house knowing John Weekes rose before dawn. He'd been aware, of course, about the relationship between her and Chas, and didn't question her decision to leave. He'd quietly driven her into Buxton to catch the early train, and gone to fetch her a coffee while she waited on the platform. But the pain and heartbreak had followed her all the way back to London.

Despite it all, she was home now, determined to ban Chas from her thoughts as she went through the flat like an automaton, opening windows, making tea in the tiny kitchen, drawing a bath, and pretending all the while, that she'd just returned from New York.

Leaving her cases for later, Sam leaned back in the tub with an herbal tea in hand, and soaked the fatigue from her bones. What little sleep she'd had during the long night had been restless, her dreams a kaleidoscope of emotion-laid images from the past ten days. It was ironic really, to have discovered her past and found the love of her life in the same place, a place where she knew she belonged, only to discover that the lord of the manor was a throwback, as ancient as the land he controlled. She'd awoken this morning in a tangle of sheets, anxious to quit Porter Hall and its pig-headed, short-sighted, cold-hearted, and arrogant owner as soon as humanly possible.

Sam scrubbed her face. She was being unfair and unkind. Chas was warm and wonderful; it just hadn't worked out in the end. But oh, it had been glorious while it lasted. Tears rolled down her cheeks as she remembered their first ride across Burton Park together, her tumble by the stream and that kiss, deep and penetrating and brooking no refusal, followed immediately by remorse and what are we getting into…their different worlds continually colliding and then merging again as the week wore on. They had come to know and to love each other with a depth that would have been impossible had they not been at Porter Hall.

Rising from the bath, Sam dried herself thoroughly, trying not to think about the feel of Chas' hands as he explored every inch of her. He had showered her with kisses and made her proud of her curvaceous physique, dismissing any of her shyness with his soft lips and firm touch. His love had unlocked her natural reserve, and for that she would forever be grateful.

Wiping the steam from the mirror, Sam took a long, hard look at herself. Same face, lightly freckled, same green eyes, thick auburn hair, and same determined chin. The dark shadows would disappear in time, but the heartbreak never would.

That she would have to live with, and she knew exactly where to start.

With the candlesticks.

Padding barefoot into the flat's teensy bedroom, Sam grabbed a pair of leggings and a t-shirt from the chest of drawers, and quickly dressed. She dug through her shoulder bag for the eleventh candlestick, which lay carefully wrapped in the same scarf she'd used to carry it from the auction rooms to Porter Hall. It might have belonged at the house at one time, but it was hers now. She hoped that whoever had owned it before her, had had a happy life. Beyond the reach of Randolph Burton-Porter and his like.

With the utmost care, she carried it into the sitting room and set it on the mantel next to her most precious belonging. They were a perfect match. Tears stung Sam's eyes. Despite all the grief she now felt, her journey had been a successful one. She knew where she came from, and how the candlestick had come to her family.

Chas had been wrong to accuse her of knowing what she was doing all along, but Sam did wonder if something she'd overheard in an unguarded moment when she was a child, had planted a seed that would one day lead her into the past. She sank into her one and only armchair and stared at the pair of candlesticks, finally united.

"You ride him any harder, he'll not thank ye," said George coming up behind Chas as he wiped the sweat from Damien's back.

Chas stiffened. The old man was right. The big chestnut loved to gallop, but Chas had driven them both faster and farther than usual.

"What brings you here?" Chas asked wearily, although he already knew the answer. The last time George had chugged his way up to the Hall on his old tractor had been the previous Christmas. This was all about Sam. In fact, everything was about Sam. Evelyn Weekes was barely speaking to him. John would tell him no more than he waited until he saw "the young lady" safely on the train. Even Max was mooning in his stall.

All because he, Chas "bloody" Porter was an arrogant idiot who'd just made a terrible mistake. So terrible, he'd driven the woman he loved out of his arms and out of his life.

When George cleared his throat, Chas tossed the damp towel into a corner. "You can't make me feel any worse than I already do, George, so just spit it out."

"Right then."

The old man pulled out his hankie and wiped his face. "I suspect you already know you're a fool, so I won't tell you again. The young lass came to see me the other day. Once she knew her Gran had worked at the Hall, she were terrified that one of them candlesticks had been stolen."

Chas grabbed a brush and began grooming Damien's flank. "My father told me it was."

"He were just a lad when all that happened," harrumphed George. "I can blame him for a lot of things, but not that. No one knew, you see. Another missing candlestick meant…"

"You don't need to remind me," snapped Chas.

"No, I don't suppose I do." George stepped forward and reached up to lay a gnarled hand on the younger man's shoulder. Chas hung his head. He'd known George his whole life; there was no room in this conversation for stubborn pride.

"Why wasn't I told the truth?"

"Your grandmother went to her grave shielding Grace and Paddy. If your grandfather, or even your father, had discovered their whereabouts, they'd have tracked them down. They were that vindictive. Don't ye see, lad? What Paddy did was unthinkable in those days. He made your grandfather the laughing stock of the valley. The old man made Eugenie's life a misery, I'll tell ye, but she stuck to her story."

"But why did she give them a candlestick?"

George dropped his hand. "Perhaps it were a bitter-sweet revenge for her husband's betrayals. A bit of summary justice. Paddy and Grace were leaving the country. Eugenie gave them what little money she had for their passage," the old farmer paused, his voice rough with emotion. "Grace was the best friend your grandmother ever had. And that young lady is her granddaughter."

"She's better off without me."

"Don't be daft," snorted George. "She tell you that?"

Damien whinnied and tossed his head. Apparently, he was in full agreement. "She might as well have," Chas mumbled. Sam's parting words had proven to him just how much he'd injured her, and himself, in the process. "I've tried calling her," he confessed to George, "but her mobile's turned off."

"Then get in that fancy car of yours and go find her."

Chas nodded, too embarrassed to reveal how little he knew about Sam's life in London. She had a flat somewhere in Notting Hill, that much he knew, but without an address, he'd be wandering the streets like the lovesick fool he was. Besides, even before George's kind counsel, Chas had made up his mind. His bag was already packed. He would drive down to London this evening, but he'd let Sam have her space tonight.

It was tomorrow he was worried about, wondering whether he'd be able to see her again without striding across the office, sweeping her into his arms and begging her forgiveness in front of the staff. He might not be as bad as his forefathers, but humble pie was best eaten in private.

Sam had decided the night before to stick to her normal routine. Shower, coffee, smart suit and out the door by eight. At exactly nine o'clock, she entered the hushed premises of Burton-Porter & Sons carrying an oversized leather briefcase. With her head held high and not a single strand of her glorious auburn hair out of place, Miss Samantha Redfern, senior silver appraiser and expert in her field, filled her lungs and strode on stage.

If she was aware of the curious eyes tracking her every move through the delicate porcelain and fine art discreetly displayed in the company showrooms, she gave no sign other than a polite nod or two in response to a colleague's friendly hello.

Once inside her office, she went directly to her corner filing cabinet and unlocked the bottom drawer. She placed the briefcase inside the drawer and slid it closed. It locked automatically.

Proud to have made it this far, Sam staggered to her desk. She had just sat down when Mia appeared in the doorway carrying a steaming mug of tea. Today's tights were striped, Sam noted with awe, the perfect foil for Mia's polka-dot sweater and Sam's black mood. "Long time no see!" trilled Mia, all wide-eyed innocence.

Sam's eyes narrowed. "Who tipped you off?"

"My buddy, Cyril. You walked right by his newsstand without even saying hello. He sent me a text."

Sam groaned. "Is there anybody in London who doesn't know?"

"Are you kidding me?" Mia walked in, handed the tea to Sam and then perched on the edge of a cherry wood side table. "This is headline news. The company's two most glamorous people shacking up together in a remote castle for days on end!" She frowned. "Hey! Wait a minute! Aren't you supposed to look happy?"

Sam felt her lower lip quiver. "Don't ask." She raised the tea to her lips and took a tentative sip. If she could just get through the day, she would be okay. The job in New York was still hers for the asking. But Mia was such a romantic at heart, if Sam wasn't careful, she would burst into tears and that would be a disaster. "So, Mia," Sam said firmly, "talk to me about anything but…you know who…" This was terrible; she couldn't even say his name out loud without fear of breaking down.

"Right," said Mia, taking her cue from Sam. "Um, nothing new on the social scene. But then when does that ever change… Miss Bossy Boots came back from New York like she was the only person who mattered…but you probably don't want to hear about that either."

Sam gave her a wan smile. "To be honest, I don't really care. But I do need you to help me keep it together in front of…" she waved her hand about, "…everybody else."

"Hey, don't worry about it. You look great and besides, who needs a…" Mia's brow creased. She jumped up and went to stand in front of Sam's desk. "I know. We'll go to that Greek place for lunch. It's really cheap…that's not why I like to go there…but the food's really good and Stavros is so cute…"

"You're babbling, Mia." And blocking my view, Sam was about to add when a deep male voice cut through her thoughts.

"Mia, can you give us a minute, please?"

A stricken Mia stared at Sam and then stepped aside to reveal the head of Burton-Porter & Sons standing in the doorway. "Miss Redfern," said Chas. "Nice to see you back in the office."

"Mr. Porter." Without shifting her gaze, Sam caught a glimpse of Mia out of the corner of her eye, her head turning from one side to another like she was watching a match at Wimbledon. "Thanks, Mia," said Sam, marveling at the steadiness in her voice, "I'll take you up on that offer later."

"Right," said Mia still entranced by the drama unfolding in front of her.

Then Chas gave her the look, and the younger woman bolted for the door.

"Business, as usual, I see," said Sam. She was glad that, like her, Chas had come to the office in full uniform. Perfectly tailored suit, crisp white shirt, silk tie and cuff links. She knew he was the same man beneath his business attire; in fact, she knew exactly what lay beneath his suit, but while he was wearing it and holding a sheaf of papers in his hand, she had a better shot at staying in control.

She pointed to the papers. "For me?"

She could tell her aloofness had caught him off-guard. His jaw tightened and his eyes changed hue, from the coolest of blues to glacier grey. The lines had been drawn. But he knew as well as she did that their private lives were on full display. Sticking to business was what they did best. Keep it professional was never more apt than today, thought Sam. Hopefully, her expression matched her resolve.

"The Manners collection. The curator is not happy with the insurance company's evaluation. He'd like you to review the paperwork and submit an independent appraisal. End of day if possible."

Sam held out her hand for the file.

Chas stepped forward, but when she grasped the file, he refused to let go. "Sam...I want to apologize and tell you how much..."

"Please, not now..." said Sam stiffly. "I couldn't bear it."

She tugged the paperwork from his hand. "I have a meeting later this morning," said Chas, "with a prospective client. And another this afternoon," he added checking his watch. "I should be back no later than five."

"The file will be on your desk."

"That's not what I meant, Sam, and you know it," said Chas. She could hear the mounting frustration in his voice.

"That's not what I meant either," whispered Sam. "Then what?"

When she didn't respond, he spun on his heel and marched out of her office. Sam yearned to go after him and half-rose from her chair, but Mia had appeared out of nowhere chasing after Chas with a chit of paper. Sam watched him take it from her and after a cursory glance, shove it in his pocket. He'd barely broken stride.

She sat back down and wearily pulled the file towards her. It would be the perfect diversion for what was bound to be the most difficult day of her life.

It was nearly six when Chas strode through the deserted showrooms at Burton-Porter, hoping against hope that the Manners account had kept Sam so busy, she'd still be in her office. Waiting for him. He'd spent most of his afternoon doodling like a school boy while the client's lawyer droned on about estate values and tax breaks. At the end of the afternoon, Chas saw that he had covered his notepad with pictures of Sam, on the terrace, in the window seat, sitting on the paddock fence.

He knew he had it bad, but never, ever had he sleep-walked through a meeting before, especially one with as much potential as this one had to swell the company coffers. It was another sign of how deeply in love he was with Samantha Redfern.

Just thinking about her made his heart race faster than a thoroughbred.

But the lights were out in her office.

Chas stood in the doorway, berating himself for thinking she'd be waiting for him. Just as she had when he'd driven back from London to find her tearing across the meadow to meet him. But this was not Porter Hall. And they were no longer an item. Either they repaired their relationship before it was too late, or they found a way to work together again.

He slung his suit jacket over his shoulder and loosened his tie. All he wanted to do was lean against the door jam, close his eyes and soak up the lingering scent of Sam's perfume. But that only made him realize how impossible it would be to spend his days this close to the woman he loved without holding her in his arms each night.

With a deep groan, he forced himself to face up to the one irrefutable fact. He couldn't live without her; he didn't want to live without her, and he certainly wasn't going to.

Decision made, he headed into his office with renewed vigor, determined to make things right, no matter what. At least he had Sam's address now, thanks to Mia. He'd call Sam first though, offer to take her out. Then beg her forgiveness. He'd even grovel if that's what it took. Anything, if only she'd give him a second chance. But when he flicked the lights on and saw what was on his desk, the briefcase slipped from his hand. Sam was gone. And in her wake, she'd left a letter with his name on it, propped against two perfectly matched silver candlesticks.

He strode to the desk, grabbed the envelope and tore it open. Inside was her resignation, and regret, that she could no longer remain at Burton-Porter & Sons. Like hell, she couldn't. Chas tore her letter to shreds, scooped up the candlesticks and stormed out of his office.

Normally, Sam enjoyed her ride home on the tube with its jostling crowds and fascinating faces, but not today. All she could think about was how loud everything seemed; the posters advertising West End theatres and high-street fashion appeared unbearably garish, and even the busker playing his violin while she'd waited on the platform, had irritated her.

Her decision to make a clean break and get on with her life should have brought relief, but she felt restless and miserably unsure of herself.

She would get off at the next station, Sam decided. Maybe walking the last few blocks to her flat would help soothe her troubled soul. But even that was a mistake. The antique and curio shops which had always drawn her in the past with their displays of fine porcelain and old silver, simply reminded her of Porter Hall.

Evelyn and John Weekes had been kindness itself, treating her with courtesy and respecting her privacy, even though when she had first arrived, she had been nothing more than another Burton-Porter employee, an unknown who had taken up with their boss. Sam quickened her step. Evelyn, in particular, deserved a heartfelt thank you for everything she had done to support Sam. In fact, she deserved a medal, but the silver pieces Sam usually picked out for her friends would not do; that was the last thing anyone at Porter Hall needed. But flowers would be perfect, thought Sam as she arrived at her neighborhood florist.

The bell over the door jangled as she stepped inside.

There was nothing quite like the heady fragrance of an abundance of blooms in a small space. Lilies, freesia and orchids competed for her attention, but with the proprietor anxious to close, Sam quickly discarded the notion of sending a cut flower arrangement. She chose a lovely white miniature rose instead, as an acknowledgement of the friendship she had shared with Evelyn in the garden. After adding a note with a promise to keep in touch, Sam left the shop with a lighter heart.

If nothing else, she had a sense of closure; but tidying up loose ends and packing her bags was the easy part. Filling the void in her heart would be a lifelong challenge. Best not dwell on it, thought Sam as she approached her building.

But once inside her flat, she realized how impossible that would be. She kicked off her shoes and curled up in her chair. She would allow herself five minutes to wallow in self-pity and then get on with it. The tiny flat was so empty.

Chas ran from the office, hailed a cab, and twenty-five minutes later was pounding up the stairs to Sam's third-floor flat with the candlesticks tucked under his left arm.

Pausing to catch his breath, Chas walked softly up the last few steps until he stood in front of her closed door. He wasn't going to back down this time. He raised his hand and knocked. Nothing. He knocked again. Louder. Still nothing. "Sam! It's me." He thumped the door with the flat of his hand. "I know you're in there."

"Go away!"

"No!"

"What are you going to do? Break down the door?"

Chas grinned. "As a matter of fact, I am… Which is what I should have done the other night!" Gritting his teeth, he took a step backwards, lowered his right shoulder and, still clutching the candlesticks, charged the door just as it swung open. He heard Sam gasp as he flew through the entrance and crashed headlong at her feet.

"A little overkill, don't you think," drawled Sam. When he answered with a groan, she dropped to the floor beside him. "Are you okay?"

"I'm fine," said Chas. He raised himself into an upright position revealing a nasty lump on his forehead and the imprint of a silver candlestick on his cheek.

"I am so, so sorry," cried Sam. "I didn't think you'd actually smash the door down."

Chas gingerly produced the candlesticks. "I believe these are yours."

"Not the candlesticks again," snapped Sam. Despite her efforts to appear angry, her eyes filled. She set the offending silver on a nearby table. "I'm beginning to have a love, hate relationship with them."

"Somewhat like ours?" Chas prodded.

"I see you got my note," said Sam.

Chas got uncomfortably to his feet. "I did, Miss Redfern, and after much consideration, have refused to accept your resignation."

Ignoring the bait, Sam grabbed a tissue from the box on the table and began to dab at his wound. "Let me get you some ice."

Chas stayed her hand with his and she went very still, her senses rising to his touch.

"Your grandparents might have been the love story my grandmother never had," he said gently, "but this is about us, Sam. We need to put the past where it belongs and trust in each other. And that includes the candlesticks."

"I have let go of the candlesticks," whispered Sam. She turned away.

Her flat was so small; it was only ten steps to the fridge. The silence was deafening above the pounding of the blood in her veins. Wanting to go to Chas. Refusing to unbend. She would not settle for anything less than the kind of love her grandparents had shared – passion laid upon a foundation of trust and deep respect.

Hands shaking, she took ice from the tray and wrapped it in a clean cloth; she didn't hear Chas come up behind her.

He slipped his arms around her waist and rested his head atop hers. "Do you know how much I love you? That I can't live without you?"

Sam nodded, letting the ice drop into the sink. She turned in his arms, looking up into the deep blue eyes that smiled into her own. There was so much to this man. He was strong and gentle, good and kind. His cold London persona was nothing more than a protective shell.

"We're not really that different," she said softly.

"No," said Chas. "I don't think we are. And it will take more than a candlestick to buy me off, Miss Redfern," he whispered. His head dropped to hers and he kissed her deeply.

A few moments later, Sam smiled up at him, eyes full of love. "So what will it take to buy you off?" she teased.

"A lifetime. You are the only woman in the world for me, Miss Samantha Redfern, and I totally adore every inch of you, including that stubborn chin of yours." He cupped her face in his hands. "Will you marry me?"

Her green eyes searched his, and liked what they saw. "I love you Chas 'bloody' Porter. With all my heart. And, yes, I will marry you." She tightened her arms around his neck and drew him closer, her lips gently parting his, claiming him as he'd claimed her.

When at last they paused, Chas was feeling more than light-headed. "You do have a bedroom, don't you?"

"I most certainly do," cooed Sam. "The bed might be small and not nearly as elegant as some I've been in, but I don't think that's going to matter, do you?"

Eugenie Grace Redfern-Porter was born eight-and-a-half months later. She has her mother's hair and her father's eyes. The tilt of her chin has yet to be determined.

A Sneak Peek at Books by
Stephanie Browning

History and mystery mingle with a great romance…impossible to put down when you want to know what comes next!
— Carole Tanner

Romance isn't on the agenda in…
Undone by the Star

As heir-apparent to one of London's most exclusive hotels, Alexis Kirkwood has spent her life preparing for the top job. But when American film star Marc Daniels saunters through the lobby of The Sadler Hotel, sparks fly.

First she mistakes him for a plumber in his scruffy jeans and work boots. And then her grandmother, The Sadler's matriarch, decides to play matchmaker.

A surprising intimacy develops…but their careers are on a collision course. Marc's a celebrity. Alex is not. Discretion is everything in her world, but she can't have it both ways. Or can she…?

Making Up is Hard to Do

If she'd known Jack Rutherford would walk back into her life, more ruggedly handsome than the day he left, Nicki Hamilton would never have agreed to run the small-town accounting firm of Gammage & Associates for the summer. She would have stayed in Toronto and left the past where it belonged.

A committed loner at thirty-four, Jack is finding everything about the lakeside community of Bedford County tantalizingly familiar. Including the pithy Miss Hamilton...but the timing isn't right. The Bedford Inn, once owned by his grandfather, is now Jack's, and what he really needs is an accountant.

Resisting the urge to throw Jack out of her office when he doesn't immediately recognize her, Nicki hides her fury and takes the job. Jack's plan to refurbish the Inn intrigues her. Besides, he owes her. Big time. For fifteen years of silence, a dozen unanswered letters, and one broken teenaged heart...

Undone by the Star

After the gentle buzz of the lobby, the intimate interior of the elevator was making Alex much too aware of the man beside her. She could see their reflection in the elevator's highly-polished brass walls. Alex was proud of her height, but she liked the fact that he towered above her. And he smelled unexpectedly good, like freshly-laundered cotton.

Her eyes slid to his mouth to find him grinning at her reflection. "Shouldn't we push the button?" he asked.

Mortified, Alex reached out and jammed the button for the fourth floor. Four times.

"That should do it."

Her eyes shot to his and stayed.

It wasn't too late to check his hands for callouses. Even a little dirt under the fingernails would be reassuring at this point. "I do hope you know what you're doing."

"Me, too."

The elevator pinged.

They had arrived.

If Marc Daniels had had any doubts about returning to England, the last fifteen minutes had proved otherwise. This could be the best gig he'd ever had. Especially watching Miss Kirkwood in action.

Marc grinned; he'd had no idea being a plumber had so many perks…like having a woman walk ahead of you in a well-tailored skirt and jacket which flattered her shape in all the right places. The colour of the fabric was good, too. Reminded him of burnished steel. He liked the contrast of that strong metallic hue against the soft white skin of Miss Kirkwood's slim wrists and elegant hands. It suited what he'd seen of her personality as well, rapier sharp with him, but courteous and kind with her elderly charges. He'd watched her shepherd them through the lobby, and the care she took matching her gait to theirs.

Now it was his turn. She led him down a silent corridor to a short hallway with a single door. The lock clicked when she swiped her card. All efficiency, she ushered him into one of the most elegant suites Marc had ever seen. And he'd been in quite a few.

"Here we are," she said. "I trust you're up for this?"

He certainly was. Whether or not he'd be able to fix the toilet was another matter.

She pointed toward a door to the right. "Over there," she said. "I'll be back to check on the repair as soon as possible."

Marc's gaze returned to the young woman. Not yet thirty, he guessed, and all done up for business. If he wasn't on the job, he thought with deep amusement, he might be tempted to trail his fingers over that lovely skin and muss her hair until she....

"You may have all the time in the world," Miss Kirkwood snapped, "but a rather important guest will be checking into this suite in less than..." she checked her watch, "...an hour."

That brought him up short. This wasn't a game for her, amusing though it was for him. He really ought to come clean, and tell her who he was. But damn it all, he'd enjoyed being in the company of a woman who didn't know what he did for a living, who treated him like a regular guy with a regular job. Well, not exactly, he smiled, remembering their exchange in the elevator. She'd obviously picked up on the same vibes he had. Unfortunately, once he revealed his true identity, those feelings would likely evaporate as quickly as they'd come, and if they didn't, it would play out in the usual fashion. They all wanted him to be the perfect, heroic guy he portrayed on the big screen, not the rather introspective, history buff he was in real life.

Although, Marc had to admit, as he eyed the delectable Miss Kirkwood, there was something he couldn't quite put his finger on that suggested she might be more interested in who he was, not what he did. The thought sent a shot of warmth through his veins.

At least it did until she raised her left arm and imperiously pointed her forefinger in the direction of the bathroom. "Anytime."

Fine, thought Marc, if that's the way she wanted to play it, then so be it. He'd jerry-rigged enough toilets in his day; why not this one? Raising his own hand in mock salute, he was searching for an appropriately sarcastic response when the toilet suddenly flushed. They stared at each other in mutual horror as the door to the bathroom swung open, and out walked what could only have been the real plumber, tools and all.

He took one look at the two of them and his jaw dropped.

"Miss Kirkwood!" he blurted, hoisting the back of his work pants up a notch with his free hand. "I didn't know you were…toilet's fixed. Needed a new flapper is all." He lumbered to a stop, took in Marc's presence and frowned. "Who would you be, then?"

Before Marc could answer, Alex had stepped forward, effectively shielding him from the other man's view. "Bert!" she addressed the plumber. "We didn't think you were available today. You know what it's like when we've got a full house. All bust and no flush. I'm afraid, I had to call for a…last-minute replacement."

"That so," said Bert craning his neck for a closer look at Marc. "Well, he certainly don't look the part."

"He doesn't, does he…?"

She's in full damage control, thought Marc in admiration. She knows something's amiss, and she's already moving to correct it.

"Do me a favour, Bert…" she was saying as she eased the plumber towards the door of the suite, "we're obviously short-staffed…why don't you sign on for the rest of the day and I'll okay your per diem."

"Right you are, Miss Kirkwood," said Bert. "Bound to be something needs doing around here." And off he went with Miss Kirkwood's blessing.

Marc was not so lucky.

The woman who rounded on him was a blaze of fury. The golden flecks in her brown eyes flashed like molten lava as she advanced towards him. "Tell me you're a con man," she demanded. "Or even better, tell me you're a jewel thief masquerading as an incompetent plumber. Or even a freelance journalist, I could forgive that; we get them all the time. Just as long as you do not tell me," she exclaimed, underscoring every word with a punch of her forefinger, "that you are the very important guest we've been expecting. Because then, I will have to regret this day for the rest of my life!"

"Why?"

"Why what?"

"Why will you regret this day for the rest of your life?" he asked.

She went very still. Her chest rose and fell as a myriad of emotions washed across her face. Their brief encounter had to have meant something to her because, Marc realized with a slight shock of surprise, it had definitely meant something to him. And for her to not know who he was had made it even sweeter. He was right to come to England, to restart his career here. Funny how this situation, this Miss Kirkwood, had suddenly chased away any doubts he may have had.

"I'm sorry," he said at last. "I put you in an awkward position."

She nodded. "So, then," she demanded, "who are you?"

Marc casually set his hold-all on the floor. *Who are you?* was not a question he normally had to answer. But then, he'd put himself in this situation, not her. She'd made an honest mistake under what he now realized were trying circumstances. While he…he'd indulged himself at her expense. He moved towards her, his hand outstretched. "Marc Daniels," he said somewhat sheepishly.

She didn't bat an eyelash; and the intriguing interplay of emotion had disappeared from her face. She held his eyes as she slid her hand in his and gave it a firm shake. "Welcome to The Sadler, Mr. Daniels," she said. "If there's anything we can do to make your stay more pleasant, please let us know." Not even a tremor in her voice. The hot-blooded woman had been replaced by the ever-so-cool professional.

And he'd thought he was the actor.

Making Up is Hard to Do

"Aachoo!" Nicki sneezed, blew her nose for the umpteenth time that day and tossed the soggy tissue into the wastebasket next to her desk. The year-end report she was preparing for the Bedford County Golf Club could go hang. She was going to go home, have a long, hot shower and crawl into bed.

"Ms. Hamilton?"

Nicki raised her red-rimmed, hazel eyes.

Madison Carswell, Gammage & Associates' young receptionist, hovered in the doorway.

"Dwat?" Nicki blew her bangs out of the way.

The receptionist frowned. "Are you okay?"

"Despite the fact that I sound like a fwrog, my hair is greasy and my nose is red enough to unseat Rudolph, I'm just tickety-boo." Nicki lobbed the half-finished report across her desk. "Dwhy, what's up?"

"There's this man..." with a slight twitch of the head, Madison indicated the reception area behind her, "...he's asking for Mr. Gammage."

Nicki sighed. She really was tired and out-of-sorts and now here was Madison, her nineteen-year-old frame practically quivering with excitement over whatever piece of male flesh waited expectantly in the outer office. "You know the drill, Madison. Tell mister whoever-he-is that Doug is on paternity leave until further notice. If the guy stills wants an accountant, he can make an appointment to see me…"

Nicki peered at the clock on the wall. It was already close to four. "Tomorrow afternoon," she said firmly. "When I am looking…and feeling better."

"But…"

"But, what?" Nicki shoved her knuckles underneath her glasses and scrubbed. Her eyes were incredibly itchy.

"It's just…he's from out-of-town."

The old-fashioned horned-rims stopped bobbing up and down. "So am I," muttered Nicki.

Madison's voice fell to a whisper. "But you've got to see this guy. He's perfect for you."

The heavy frames dropped back into place. "I know this is a small town, Madison." Nicki said carefully, "but being thirty-one and single is not a crime. At least, not where I come from. Now go back and tell him…"

She reached for her appointment book and flipped it open.

"…that I can see him…"

Nicki never did discover what made her look up just then, but as she did, Madison shifted to one side of the doorway, leaving Nicki with a clear view of the man in the outer office.

He wasn't quite as gorgeous as her enthusiastic receptionist had suggested, but there was definitely something about the way he stood with his back to them, discreetly watching the traffic crawl along Main Street while he waited, that captured Nicki's attention.

And held it while she took in the broad sweep of his shoulders, the crisp lines of his tan chinos and the cotton shirt he so casually wore. She pegged him at about thirty-four or five. Unlike her own salon-styled highlights, which looked fabulous when freshly washed and disastrous when not, his sandy brown hair shone as though it had been touched by the sun. It was long enough to nudge the edge of his collar, but well cut so that it stayed in line. Except for one stray curl, a tiny cowlick determined to go its own way.

Nicki felt her fingers twitch in recognition. "Psst! Madison!" she whispered hoarsely, beckoning the receptionist closer. "Did he say where he's from?"

"Yeah. Watertown."

"As in New York?" Nicki squeaked. Her voice sounded as though it had risen an octave.

"Uh, yeah."

Nicki frowned. She knew the Lake Ontario town of Eastport was crawling with tourists this time of year, many of whom were American. Besides, she reminded herself, half the population of Bedford County had family and friends on both sides of the border, some of whom spent as much time in New York as they did here.

The trouble was none of them ever made her palms sweat or her heart lurch with sudden longing the way this man did.

"He didn't happen to tell you his name, did he?"

"Um, Ruther-something, I think."

For a split-second, Nicki felt her world go black around the edges.

Not Ruther-something. Rutherford. Jack. Born Syracuse, New York. Mother American, father Canadian. Summers spent in Bedford County. Heart given to teenaged girl. Undying love given to him in return. Three passionate letters exchanged. A dozen more sent.

And then nothing.

For fifteen long years.

Nicki blinked.

Madison was speaking to her. "What do you want me to do?"

Short of telling Jack Rutherford to go away until she could whip home, wash her hair, put her contacts back in and lose five pounds, there was nothing Madison could do.

"Give me two minutes," Nicki said firmly. "And then show him in."

Damn. This was not the way it was supposed to happen. She should have been sitting in a sidewalk café sipping an espresso, or strolling along the Champs-Elysées on a beautiful spring day wearing an elegant dress and a wide-brimmed hat.

It was too late now.

Nicki breathed in deeply, tucked a lank strand of hair behind one ear, and moistened her lips with her tongue. She grabbed her summary page on the golf course and tried to study it, but her hands were shaking so badly, the carefully prepared columns seemed to morph into a solid block of black ink.

And then, suddenly, Jack was there, filling the doorway to her office. He seemed taller somehow. At least six-foot-two from where she was sitting, and he'd filled out. Everywhere. In the way a man does when he earns his muscles the hard way.

"Ms. Hamilton?"

His accent had softened. From upstate New York to somewhere neither here, nor there. With great deliberation, Nicki set the papers she was holding on top of the desk, and rose to her feet. The moss-green summer suit she wore nipped in at the waist and flattered her full figure, but the skirt, which stopped just short of her knees, did nothing to hide the tremble in her legs as she walked towards him.

Jack was smiling politely, holding out his hand.

"Jack Rutherford."

"Mr. Rutherford." Nicki broke out in a grin. Now that he was this close she could see the tiny lines radiating from the corners of his incredible blue eyes, and she found herself wondering where the intervening years had taken him.

"Thank you for seeing me on such short notice."

She stared at his hand for a moment, caught short by the formality of his greeting, and then she slipped her hand in his.

It was warm, and slightly calloused. She could feel the strength in his grip. It sent a delicious signal of familiarity to every nerve in her body. The yearnings of a sixteen-year-old girl roared to the surface of the woman she had become.

Swallowing her tears of happiness, Nicki raised her glance to his once more. He stared down at her and she started, suddenly reminded of how truly revealing the colour of Jack's eyes could be. From sky blue to cobalt and back again depending on his mood.

A sharp chill, as cold and grey as liquid mercury, rippled through Nicki's veins. It wiped the goofy grin from her face and sent her heart into overdrive.

Jack Rutherford, the man she had loved unconditionally for nearly half her lifetime, had no idea who she was.

About the Author

Anne Stephenson and Susan Brown met at Carleton University in Ottawa, where they discovered that not only were they both in journalism, they were sharing the same teeny, tiny dorm room. It could have been a disaster, but once the sleeping arrangements had been sorted out, they quickly became fast friends, sharing many excellent adventures. They did not realize when they graduated and went their separate ways, it would be years before they saw each other again. When they finally did meet up, with husbands and children in tow, they decided, over a glass of chilled chardonnay, to continue their adventures and write together.

Enter Stephanie Browning

One part Anne, one part Susan, their perfect persona is having a blast writing romances for women who care deeply about love, honour, friendship and courage without ever losing sight of the finer things in life…like a well-toned physique, a powerful set of shoulders and a pair of eyes that can rake a woman at fifty yards.

With Outbid by the Boss and Undone by the Star already capturing readers' hearts, Susan and Anne are breaking new ground on this side of the Atlantic with a steamy story of lovers reunited. Set in the lakeside community of Bedford County, Making Up is Hard to Do will leave you wanting more….

Because love isn't just for city folk, it's for small-town girls, too!

Susan Brown
www.susanbrownwrites.com

Anne Stephenson
www.annestephensonwriter.com